The LOVE I Know

STEED PUBLISHING

ISBN: 978-0-9964293-0-6

10 9 8 7 6 5 4 3 2   0 1 0 8 1 6

Illustrators:
Phillip Alexander
Kareem Kenyada,
Munson Steed

Printed in the United States of America

∞This paper meets the requirements of ANSI/NISO Z39.48-1992
(Permanence of Paper)

The LOVE I Know

A Collection of Love Stories to be Shared and Read Aloud

MUNSON W. STEED

STEED PUBLISHING

This book is dedicated to my mother, my wife and my team.
I thank God who loved me before I even knew the word.

FROM THE AUTHOR

In the male-female love tragedy, we discover that both genders are ultimately dependent upon each other. Through the journey of love, we are expected to grow and evolve into a wiser human. One that can identify and articulate what we require emotionally. So often, Love is assumed and not expressed enough or clearly and that non-verbalized miscommunication of expectations and/ or needs can lead to the tragic lost of an emotional investment. During this demise, there are fleeting voices that echoes in our heads about a fairytale not realized and emotions that sometimes can only be overcome through counseling. From love lost, we reveal our true selves and highlight who we are, what we believe, what we deserve and how to love and to be loved. The Love I Know is an artistic interpretation of love in various creative voices that reverberate from the urban street corners to Wall Street. The intent is to help people engage in discussions that will eliminate statements of; I didn't know you felt that way or I didn't know you needed that type of love or behavior from me. To hopefully prevent less heartbreaks and Spark the fulfillment of each person's emotional wants, desires and the needs of love required to navigate this life.

CONTENTS

Preface	8
Language Barriers	11
Cooley's Angel	23
Love Me Forever	43
Invisible Keys to Forever	50
The Inside of You	64
If You Reach for It	73
I'll Always be Looking at You	93
Wall Street Woman	111
Melt	125
Knock	138
The Bowl of Icing	153
Fasten Your Seatbelts	170
Love Someone	172

PREFACE

The love we know is often defined by what we don't know: Will he call? Does she see me? Am I ready to make a commitment? Is the timing right? Will I ever find true love? These questions are just a few of the countless ones men and women ponder as they maneuver the landscape of love and relationships. In his collection of short stories, *The Love I Know*, Munson Steed offers glimpses into the lives of everyday people who are defining their individual paths to love. He allows us to see through their eyes and experiences the intrigue, the vulnerability, the magic, the disappointment, the surprise, the tenacity and ultimately the power of love.

Many of these scenarios focus on the development of relationships and the hope and fulfillment yet to be realized. But each story reveals that relationships require focus, energy and commitment—surprising or not—the same type of energy that one gives to a job or vocation. Though the backdrops may change from busy inner city hustle to the idyllic walkways of a college campus to a church pulpit, Steed allows us to enter the lives of each of his characters with the same intent—to accompany them on their path of discovery. Through his eyes, we become both friend and observer. He allows us to witness critical turning points in his characters' lives. While we may already know the consequences of the roads not taken, Steed provides readers key moments along the path for his characters to choose or they're chosen for them. We learn as they learn.

Language Barriers—Share your passion in any language you speak.

Cooley's Angel—The past does not always predict your future. However, if you learn from the past and live to tell the tale, your story, it may be summarized in these few words: God does give second chances.

Love Me Forever—A mother's love comes in all kinds of packages —but one thing for sure, it's the forever kind of love.

Invisible Keys to Forever—Two brothers traveling their own paths to success a strong family bond allows for inclusion of others.

The Inside of You—Although "*The Inside of You*" is shared through the eyes of a an artist, it depicts a woman who needs to stop and see the beauty that surrounds her. The couple finds what they've both been missing.

If You Reach for It—Believe that first love is forever love.

I'll Always be Looking at You—One model's beauty captured through the perfect lens of a photographer. Yet she longs to show her whole self through the eyes of love.

Wall Street Woman—Is it all about the numbers?

The Bowl of Icing—If you appreciate the rewards that hard-earned effort can bring then you should also treat yourself to the sweet little indulgences of life. You may be surprised at what it will offer.

The Love I Know shares with its readers the joy and promise of first love and the satisfaction of the waited-for love. It offers a vast array of conversations on possibilities of love. Some of vignettes lean toward eroticism; while others uncover the reason an individual is reluctant to make that first move. All of the stories move toward the next answered question. Will tonight be the night? Will it last? Am I crazy or what? Even when we are left to decide our own conclusions—we are left with the hope and promise of love.

LANGUAGE BARRIERS

You were sitting at the desk in front of me that first day. I noticed your soft, round shoulders. Your glowing skin had the scent of cocoa butter and lavender oil. You looked to the left to smile and say hello to a friend. You were so elegant.

I was the only man in the class—a transient who dared to cross into the all female territory to sit in the back of a classroom at an all-girls school. That was 22 years ago and I still remember vividly.

You had this way of moving: gracefully with your chin up and head back in a perfect line. Your comportment whispered you were a dancer, a debutante, and possibly belonged to a group of polished people. I began to learn something about women, beauty and hair. I stared into this natural, bold collection of tight, oval curls. No straightener. Not quite locked but naturally gathering, and seeming to call me to touch. I was drawn to do so, but I knew better.

Who would've known that natural hair would become the rage?

Others around me darted for those women who represented other things that they found society declares appealing—the designer wearer; long, silky hair; the natural red head with pale skin; or the girls who pledged to some particular group or organization. They sort out those things, but I was sitting behind you, and saw a vision of beauty.

I remember the second day when you turned around to me and smiled. You hair was in two long, chunky braids, both resting on your left shoulder. I thought to ask your name, but I was too late. You were already done with me. The girl who sat beside us in a tangerine sundress, the one who'd drop the class after two days, needed a pen.

You unbuckled your bag and reached inside. I realized you hadn't really parted your hair, but gathered it on either side, the middle a sea of ruffles that looked like someone took time to touch them.

I looked and watched. You handed her the pen. You buckled the bronze clasp. You turned around and smiled again. You asked my name.

"Chris," I answered.

You asked if I was up to the challenge of the class.

I answered simply, "Sí."

We both laughed.

We were students in Dr. Celestina's advanced Spanish class. I'd heard she could speak fifteen languages fluently. On the first day of class, she admitted it was only seven, but only one she liked to teach. Spanish, she said, was the language of romance—the language of touch. There were no barriers. Just feeling.

She partnered each student. It looked like a third grade class or some high school biology lab—a space filled with women holding index cards, hiding the names of unfamiliar faces they had to find.

I read the name on my card with anticipation that it was yours, but realized I hadn't asked your name. And not knowing how fortunate I was, I stammered around trying to look like I was doing something like mingling as I asked for names in a weak Spanish that barely survived my Mississippi drawl.

You came straight to me.

"It reads 'Christopher,' Chris." You turned the card so I could see and winked at me through tortoise shell glasses that said "I'm smart."

When we sat down, Dr. Celestina gave more insight on the assignment. We'd been paired according to our levels of competence and understanding of the language, our ability to communicate. There were words she wanted each of us to know and share—to say to each other.

"You are very special and I picked someone very special for you," Dr. Celestina said to me when I went to her office after class. It was the first of ten private meetings I'd have with her. We were to speak only in Spanish, but the praise, the first thing she'd said when I walked in the door, was in English.

She asked what I'd read and gave me more books than I could carry. While stuffing one in my pocket and another beneath my arm, I shared with her that I had just finished a class on Don Quixote, and that perhaps I'd overused a Miguel de Cervantes quote while leaning in to impress young señoritas.

"I know who I am and who I may be if I choose."

She laughed and rolled backwards her head full of loose, dark brown curls that fell to her shoulders and cascaded down her back. "Chévere, I hope in time you will find windmills to conquer."

She explained how the Spanish language changed over time and the necessity of siestas. There were moments in time when even a poor boy could find sleep and an old woman, her vanilla skin withered by the sun on the horizon, could find hours of happiness. There were moments that stood still and gave age, time and love reverence.

At our second meeting, she began to weave you into this timeline, sharing with me how I should learn Spanish from you. I should enjoy watching your mouth say the words since you enunciated and spoke them so clearly. I should listen, should keep my eyes open, repeat the words in my heart and say what first came to me.

And then it was time for us to study together. Of course, I resided off campus, a bus ride and short walk away, but you stayed in a dorm, what you called "a wonderful hall" built for freshmen in the early 1900s that was now inhabited by juniors and seniors who stayed on campus to avoid traveling through the sprawling city and endure unwanted encounters. You said on the phone that you were an RA, and had your own room in a charming attic with a window, a balcony and a built-in desk.

I remembered all of this. I thought to comment on each in Spanish when I walked in the door—the attic was delightful, the balcony romantic, and the desk a beautiful antique. You'd be impressed and maybe ask me to sit on the bed, which you said was a wall pull-out. But when I walked in, I had to request to see you. Visitors were only allowed downstairs, and while you were an RA and had special privileges, you kept me downstairs that first time. The delightful attic and romantic balcony and beautiful antique desk would have to wait as other brothers passed us sharing our Spanish flash cards in the study room, calling on girls in shiny, freshly polished Mary Janes so they could walk across campus or out to dinner or to a movie.

We were talking about words, sharing the words Dr. Celestina outlined for us. I watched you wrap your hair in a turquoise mud cloth and thought of something she'd said about time.

"Chévere," you said, looking at me. And I heard you. I repeated it in my heart and uttered the first thing that came to mind.

"Chévere."

I wanted to stop this time. To remember your hands twisting the turquoise scarf, the curve of your lips and the sun setting outside of the window.

"When you enunciate words, you draw people into your life—into your experience. They can touch your soul and you can touch theirs. You will find that you want to be inside the very place where the words are being spoken. You want to go in and have them expressed in temperatures that are beyond 98 degrees. You want to become the human thermometer to gauge the temperature and understand the beauty of those words. You want to be touched like the words that linger on the lips as they are enunciated." This is what Dr. Celestina said to me in Spanish at our fourth meeting. I was still on the other side of her desk, but she seemed closer somehow. The office wasn't very big. There was only enough space for two chairs, a filing cabinet, the oak desk, and us.

I couldn't move. She kind of twirled and she darted about in my face, and then she seemed even closer by leaning her head in her hand on the desk. Her chair was on the side of the desk. And then next to mine. When she laughed, it seemed like she was dancing. She kind of twirled and she darted about in my face, and next leaning her head and hair in her hand on the desk.

At our fifth meeting, she asked if I had extra time, and before I could answer, she reached past me and adjusted a needle to wax on a cheap, green record player.

The music was bad, but sexy. Her dress was loose and falling off of her shoulders. She said words to me, got close to my face and then twirled away. Her neck turned red with splotches of white. She closed the door and turned the volume up. She surprised me with new words, words that men say to women in Spanish, the language of love. And then she told me, "Think of me when you're with your partner. Think of me when you say the words to her, and think of my body dancing in front of and around you."

I could finally use my words to describe your special room in the attic. We became comfotable and your pink fingernails summoned me up a back staircase to study.

"What kind of name is Anastasia for a Black girl?" I offered a joke and you laughed.

"The kind I have." You stuck out your tongue and it was the first time I'd ever seen you act so silly.

I moved closer on the bed.

I remember how your eyes looked liked pools of Coca-Cola with the sun streaming into the window. For a second, I didn't remember what I was there to study.

We listened to First Take, Roberta Flack along with some songs written by Donnie Hathaway.

You told me "The First Time Ever I Saw Your Face" was the loveliest song you'd ever heard, and I saw in your eyes you meant it.

You played it four or five more times as I tried to inch closer.

My lips were so close to your brown and elegant neck and I wanted so much to just fall.

"I have a boyfriend," you said, turning and looking over at me as the song stopped again. My heart stopped, too. That truth was like a kick in my chest and I dared not say what first came to my mind. You must've seen me then—frozen.

I warmed up after when you looked into my eyes and said the two of you weren't getting along very well. You talked about the feeling, the connection you felt with me, but you didn't want to get involved without me knowing about him.

I didn't want to know anything though. It was a conflict of interest for me. I'd never been good at sharing—not red balls or green action figures, not someone as beautiful as you.

By my seventh meeting with Dr. Celestina, I'd memorized her dancing, how close her seat would get to mine and exactly where on her blushing neck the white spots would appear. I wondered if she treated all of her students this way. I wondered if I'd always remember these moments in the small office with my advanced Spanish professor. My pants tightening, hidden underneath my textbook. Her hands threatening to pull it away as she reached for the record player. I felt like most men do when they want to disappear because of their lack of control and the realization they're being led and there's so little they can do about it.

And when she told me to stick my tongue out and she stuck hers out too, I was flabbergasted. I felt something should stop and go all at the same time. I knew I had to stay in my seat although she was out of hers, instructing me to roll my tongue in and out to make a proper Spanish "R" sound. She looked at my hands, folded tightly over the textbook on my lap. "Don't forget to do your homework and study tonight," she said, turning the music off suddenly. "Meet with your partner and think of me."

In class, Dr. Celestina read love stories. She seemed so alone in front of the room, staring, seemingly lost in some affair she remembered and still longed for.

"Dueles la luz mi Corazón. Corazón—heart. Dueles la luz—you are the light."

I remembered this. And would say it one day to someone when it was true.

It wasn't my day to meet with her, but I went to Dr. Celestina's office after class that day. I told her about your "el nuvio"— the boyfriend.

She was good about it and read poems of how love sometimes

came at night when flowers blossomed and dew gathered along the tips of blades of grass.

She told me a story about a woman loving a man, and sometimes two and sometimes being loved back by more. She talked about how men pursued love and pursued her. She said not to worry about the boyfriend. I would find a way.

"Solo dos—only two," she said, telling me to repeat the words. She touched my face and pulled my hand from the top of my textbook. She looked into my eyes.

"Ahora mismo—right now."

She was so close. I could feel her breath on my lips and the hands that groped and stroked my head fell away and landed lightly on my shoulders.

"Mi cuervo mi body para ti."

I touched her—pushed my hand between her legs, closer to the knees, and felt her exhale. She slid down in her seat, leaning over to me like I leaned into you. Our lips came together and we were kissing.

"Ahora mismo, right now."

This was not a high school petting session or even two college kids making out. This was beyond, far beyond any of my previous exploits. I learned things about myself when I touched and held her and thought of you. And when our bodies parted, your gentle fingers touched my lips and you whispered, "Gracias. Thank you."

In session eight, Dr. Celestina asked me where we were. She was wearing red lipstick and her eyelashes were clumped together from too much mascara.

"Does she still have one boyfriend or can she love two, like now? Ahora mismso." She told me to repeat the words to her. She pulled her blouse down below her shoulders and said, "Say it to me now."

What was I to do?

"Ustedes son la luz de mi corazón."

She turned back toward me and said, "Say it again."

She got up, pressed her back against the door and turned the lock.

"Ustedes son la luz de mi corazón, tambien. You are the light of my heart also."

I wondered what would come next.

She leaned against the wall and instructed me to close my eyes and describe the feeling to her.

She said, "I've known all along. I can feel it, too."

The books were no longer in my lap.

I wanted her to know.

I looked into her eyes. Maybe she thinks I'm naïve, but I'm not. Or maybe she needs to know that this is research for her book.

I closed my eyes and described what maybe it would be like to kiss her. To speak into her. To be inside of her. The kiss and detail.

I told her I felt heat. I told her I never wanted the feeling to end.

She wrapped her arms around her waist and clutched herself. She rushed to the door and swung it wide open.

I thought she was dismissing me again, so I stood up, but she quickly slammed the door shut. She pushed me against the wall face first, and pressing herself against me, whispered in my ear from behind, "Ustedes son la luz de mi corazón." It feels like we're dancing.

She wrapped her arms around me and told me, "Enjoy every moment that you can. Let there not be a moment when love touches you and you don't take time to embrace it and experience it. Take it and hold it in your soul, and wrap yourself in it. Feel it deeply and feel it truly. Make it live in you. Burn yourself with it and feel your flesh under the heat. Feel every deliciously painful and excruciatingly wonderful moment. Ustedes son la luz de mi corazón, la luz de mi corazón. You are the light of my heart, the light of my heart. Eres mi vida. You are my life." She squeezed me and turned me around. "Besarme ahora. kiss me now." She kissed me on the forehead, turned me toward the door and said, "Be away."

At the end of that semester, you reminded me you had a boyfriend. We were sitting closely on the bed again, pretending to be studying for a final exam. Your hair was locking. You changed your major to Spanish. You were crying and probably saying something about him or me, but all I could hear was talk about forever.

I visualized him doing to you what I had done to her.

I wondered if he whispered Spanish in your ear.

"Chévere. I know who I am and who I may be if I choose."

He couldn't hear you the way I heard you.

"What should I do? Should I tell him?" You asked, placing my hand on your heart.

"Tell the truth in Spanish," I said.

People were talking. Dr. Celestina's husband surprised her with a new life in Peru. She quit via telegram and even left her green record player in that office for me. Red ink on a sticker spelled out my name.

It was after Christmas break. I was holding that green record player in my hands as I walked toward your dorm.

You hadn't come by. You hadn't called. But I thought, maybe.

The girl with the tangerine sundress—the one from class—was sitting at a desk.

She told me you'd moved off campus. She looked at the record player.

"You're Christopher. Right? Was that your Roberta Flack record she left up there?"

COOLEY'S ANGEL

"My cups runneth over" were the words etched on a wrought iron gate at the entrance of Bishop Cooley's Bible College. The message intrigued passersby.

The campus was two blocks long. The mouth of the gilded white gate welcomed Cadillacs with smoky windows and Rolls-Royces, license plates-free. High above was a security tower with ornate stained glass tile and Roman columns that could make any mosque in Mecca or a cathedral in Rome envious.

But this was Cooley's Place in Chicago. Envy wasn't necessary. Extravagance was not only accepted, it was expected. Those driving by were happy to get a glimpse and only envisioned what lies beyond the white gate on East Drive.

"That sign ain't right—is it Momma?" a son sporting a fresh Easter haircut asked his mother. He'd finished only half of his catechism lessons, obviously.

The mother—wearing white gloves, a white hat and bright red toenail polish hidden beneath her white shoes—remained silent. She waved at the guard in the tower and pulled her child by his coat sleeve.

"There ain't no 's' in cup. Not in the Holy Bible. I saw it in Sunday school." The son goes on, ignoring his mother's haste.

"That's Cooley," she answers after they enter the gates. "And that's right."

"You can't change the Bible," the son insists proudly and with conviction, poking out his chest like his Sunday school teacher. "God's word is God's—"

"He ain't changed God's word. He changed his life. He's changed many men's lives—proved to them that they could."

"How he do that?"

"Well, they say he had two lives himself. Two separate lives with their own deaths. Two souls," she said and stopped to look at her son. "You understand? Two hearts. Two cups. And he had to choose."

"How'd he get two lives when most men only get one? How Momma?"

"They say the Bishop prayed." She took his hand and squeezed it just enough so he'd always remember the moment he heard Cooley's story. "He came up on the devil one night in a dream and realized he was looking in the mirror. They say he said he doesn't ever remember waking up either. He just started running. Running and praying to God that he wasn't no devil. That he could be something else."

"What did God do?" The boy asked, seeing in his mind the Blackest man running down the blackest street in the blackest night.

"Sent him an angel. That's what they say. God sent Bishop Cooley an angel."

— The Angel's Request

When the story began, it was June and Atlanta was on fire—not just the temperature, but with energy. The sun was only as far away as the tin rooftops. And the brown faces in Mechanicsville were enjoying an air-conditioned escape inside of their shotgun houses, while others were out and around the streets, scattered about and rolling like marbles in a box.

Something was going to happen. Heat like this could only mean that. People were frustrated, angry, looking for a distraction, something, anything to get away, if only for a second, from the reality of an oppressive heat that turned men to beasts and women to moving prey.

When Cooley's long black Cadillac came creeping around the corner, his thoughts his women went right into motion. Hands on hips. Legs poked out over the curb. Purring. Negotiating. Hopping into cars. Walking into alleys. Bargaining what they had to get what was his.

The windows were down, air conditioner turned off, but Cooley was cool. He dangled his hand outside the window wearing a big white hat. A white wide-collared shirt. No shades. He wanted to see. Angel saw him and instead of moving, she stopped. Looking toward the car and smiling as if she was admiring something that belonged to her. She'd been standing out there, moving around on the street corner for more hours than her feet could carry and Cooley's Cadillac appeared like a blessing. It was right on time and looked like a lemonade stand on a long and hot, dusty country road. The mirage faded when another girl called Sugar waved for her to get moving.

"You better get on, country girl," Sugar said as Cooley approached the curb where they were hovering near the chicken stand. "A man ain't never nice for long. He needs what he wants."

Cooley had been nice to Angel for so long, weeks now, but that was always the way with the new girls. He'd have to break her soon. And Sugar thought it was in order to save Angel from seeing the fire in a devil she probably thought was God. It was no use though. She saw in Angel's soft eyes a girl who thought she could change a man with prayer and love. A tragic wish. He'd change her first.

"But my feet hurt," Angel whined playfully, smiling and waving at the front of the Cadillac. She turned to suggest that Sugar escape the heat with her and ask Cooley to take them for a ride—not far, to Auburn Avenue and back—but Sugar was gone, half-walking, half-running to hop into the car of a regular who'd stopped a ways up.

Angel couldn't feel all of the eyes on her when she walked toward the Cadillac. She couldn't hear the silent warnings telling her to move on, go away, run, make an excuse, say anything until you had, for sure, all of what was his.

"Hey, Daddy," Angel said with a girlish wink, stepping toward the open passenger-side window.

The men in the barbershop across the way could see that Cooley hardly smiled. His thick, jet black mustache barely moved when he said, "Put your head in the window; I've got something to tell you."

"Don't do it," Old Walter, the man who'd stopped turning the chicken in the stand, said in far too low an octave for Angel to hear.

25

She'd been standing in front of the place since he opened after the club let out on Friday morning. Hadn't left one time. No way did she have what was his. No way he was simply gonna let her off.

"Country girl, no. Don't do that. Don't put your head in that car," Old Walter commanded, but again it was too low. It wasn't his business to say it louder. At that time, at that place, men didn't get into other men's business—especially not Cooley's business.

Angel leaned into the car.

"You got my money?"

She dropped a handful of sweaty dollar bills from her breasts onto the empty red leather passenger seat.

The guys in the barbershop saw that Cooley finally smiled. There was a collective sigh.

He pulled his hand from the window, wiped a few beads of sweat from beneath his chin and politely raised the window up on Angel's neck. He took the car out of park, pressed his foot lightly on the gas, and engaged his mouth in a scolding that was an especially vile berating that no child of God could ever repeat. Angel's face from outside the car looked like a fish trapped in a catcher's net. Barely holding on, hands pressed against the glass hoping to find relief. Wig flopping down her back. High heels skittering on the concrete. Halter top sliding down. Breasts popping out. She screamed for God first and after realizing he wasn't driving the car, she screamed for Cooley next. She loved Cooley. Admired him. And wasn't she his best girl? Didn't he love her?

Cooley kept his foot on the gas pedal and told her, "You were right the first time. You need to call on God cause your country-Tupelo-Mississippi-ass is getting ready to pay the price for the absence of a fucking brain...and my money."

The people ran out the shops into the street, jogging behind the Cadillac. Some begged Cooley to stop, others watched the sad spectacle, a few just wanted to see what would happen next.

"JEEZUS!" Angel, whose real name was Lita Ann Wheeler, cried out like her Memaw did when they found Lita's mother's dead body cut up and swollen in a beaver dam on the "WHITES ONLY" side of the river.

The noise knocked against every surface in that Cadillac and Cooley took his foot off the gas pedal and looked at Angel. The car came to a slow, rolling stop. The people behind it froze a few feet back.

It was at this very moment that Angel saw in Cooley's pointy eyes a devil that had been hidden when he arrived on her Memaw's steps in Tupelo, agreeing to take her to Chicago to have a good Christian life and spread the good news to whomever would listen—they needed to stop in Atlanta, he'd said, make some money, clear up some things, so they'd have an easier way. This big man in a suit, this stranger who said he loved God and wanted to dedicate his life to Him, was everything she'd prayed for in church, was everything God said He'd send her in a husband. So, it didn't take much for her to hop shotgun into that Cadillac with nothing but her grandmother's Bible and her mother's old shoes in a brown paper bag.

Cooley pressed the release button like he was putting a nickel into the collection plate and the window began to roll down with Angel's hands still pressed against it.

She leaned back, clearing her way from the door, grabbed at her neck and gasped for more air before fixing her halter top. She kept her eyes on his, though. She wanted to see something. Wanted to know and believe that he was still that good man she'd met in Tupelo. She pulled the last pin from her wig and let it fall into the street. A stocking cap covered a head of thick, brown curls that poked out at her ears.

"I'm a child of God. And if the spirit is in me, Cooley, it's inside of you," she started, still crouched over. "You have prayed many a nights with me and I know that this shit on the street done confused your mind and the devil done led you to believe that your life ain't good without having him in your life. But I swear to God that's not all you are. I swear to God, Cooley, that as I worked these streets, I've tricked more people in my life fast-talking like you told me to do, clipping and slipping everybody out of something that I never had, and all for you. All because I believed. I've been a devil in this situation. Waiting for you to come to your common sense. Waiting for you to be the man who you said you are when you took me from

the place you say made me so stupid. I've been waiting for you to make a difference in my life."

She stammered and opened the car door, digging her knee into the seat, and pointing into Cooley's eyes as she spoke to him without fear. "You're not about to kill me in these streets—not like some chicken having his head pulled off in the middle of the country for everybody else to eat." She banged on the steering wheel and every-

one gathered in the street behind the car waited for Cooley to hit her. "You said you needed me. You took me. So now I'm yours. And I done got you your money. Didn't I? And I'll be damned that you ain't going to marry me and take me to Chicago like you said you was, so we can start your Bible College like you told my Memaw."

"I ain't told that old toothless cow nothing I ain't mean," Cooley spat, but he was cool as a Ball jar filled with ice and sweet tea. "And

I damn sure ain't about to marry you, but you can sit your crazy ass down in that seat and the schoolin' that I'm getting ready to give you is getting ready to come from a man."

"Stop talkin' to me like you're a pimp," Angel scolded him. "The Word of Jesus is upon me and I rebuke the spirit out of you. You is not a pimp. You's a damn altar boy! You going to be a preacher, a deacon, you gonna be a bishop. That's the calling on your life. Maybe you done forgot. Maybe you thought I forgot—but I ain't. I'm still Lita Ann. And you still Bernard Cooley. And Bernard Cooley promised me, told me you was called by God, used God's name to make me come with you. So, you need to come out of that bag that you're in and take me to Chicago and marry me."

Angel twisted and turned and sat in the seat. Slammed the door shut and crossed her arms over her breasts. Cooley pushed his hand back out the window, pressed his foot on the gas and the car started moving—right over the wig at first, but then over the railroad tracks and then right onto the highway.

The people stood out in the street for a minute, but figured the Cadillac wasn't ever going to stop.

— The Executioner's Good Deed

But it did stop. When the sun had gone down and blackness took over the night, Cooley's eyes were burning with sweat, so he pulled the car off the highway leading a ways north and a ways west, into a rest stop where "WHITES ONLY" signs marked territory at every turn.

"Where are we, Bernie?" Lita mumbled as she awakened slowly, her eyes forced half open.

"A few hops from the Georgia border, I think," Cooley answered her.

"Where?" Lita's voice was clear now, mixed with surprise and fear. She popped up and looked around and out the windows. The one light up over the stop house dropped a dim glow over a sprinkling of a few raggedy cars with sleeping White passengers tucked inside. She could see the tops of their lazy blond, red and brown heads. Her throat tightened. "We can't be here. Are you crazy?

They wake—anybody wake—and we dead. They gonna kill us."

"I need a few winks. Get my mind right, my thoughts steady, so I can figure this thing out—how we gonna get all the way to Chicago," Cooley said, reclining in his seat and preparing for rest. He was lying, though. He had pulled over to rest, to think, but really the thought at the front of his mind was turning back. Chicago was some shadowy dream Lita believed God sent her. She talked about it so much he almost thought God had spoken to him too. She'd been at it again since they'd left the crowd at the chicken stand. After a few minutes of quiet in the car and the calm coming with the breeze, she started talking to him and about his destiny again. "You're supposed to build something big and special in Chicago. You're not the only pimp or hustler that needs to find a way to be a preacher for God. You'll figure it out. We did what you wanted in Atlanta, and now you got your money. Don't ask me to stand on nothing else," she said. "I'm going to be a secretary for you and a wife. That's when you will marry me."

Cooley looked at her. She had the softest almond colored hands he'd ever seen. He couldn't imagine not seeing them. Never seeing her. He knew that even a country girl from Tupelo would have the proper sense to leave a man who couldn't make good on his promises—even if she'd come up with them. But still, he wasn't convinced that he wasn't really a pimp. Pimp Cooley. That's who he was before he'd met her. Maybe that's who he'd be after. He could talk his way out of anything, but he couldn't pretend. Couldn't fake what she wanted him to do, what he knew was best to do.

He fingered the ring that he kept inside the sweatband of his hat, next to the Dobbs insignia. He could ask her to marry him. She would cry. Say yes. He could wait it out then, after she was confident, knew whose she was. But he wasn't sure.

"Here I am, ain't never been to Chicago, ain't never been married. Here I am, God; talk to me now. I need to hear something," he said when he saw the sign for the rest stop.

Lita was sleeping then, and he didn't hear anything from God, so he pulled over. He had to make his own decision. Chicago was big, far away, money might be hard to make. It was a dream on a wrinkled

map. He knew and understood Atlanta. It was behind them, as small
as a baby's shoe in Cooley's mind and that's where money fell off the
vine like fat tomatoes in a new garden. He'd take a nap, wake up and
drive back to the Mechanicsville neighborhood where he was king.
He'd drive back while Angel was still asleep. But she woke up before
he could turn around.

"They're gonna kill us," Lita repeated, her eyes locked on the
quiet parked cars, her mind seeing her mother's puffy body in the
beaver dam.

"Ain't nobody gonna die. We'll be up and out of here before anybody wakes up."

"When are they going to wake up?" Lita pushed him.

"Look, woman, stop giving me this talking to. I said we gonna
leave soon after I get my rest. I'm with you and that's safe as you
gonna get. Ain't this what you wanted?"

Lita couldn't hear Cooley at all. In her mind there was only waking
and evil White faces, girls with sticks, boys with rocks, women with
nasty words, men with ropes, her mother's neck cut, her body naked
and raw with sores.

"But we ain't dressed," she said, pulling the stocking cap off her
head. "Ain't decent." She looked at Cooley's hat and shirt sitting
neat on the backseat.

His hair was knotty and the heat had forced him to remove the
shirt an hour ago. He was wearing a sleeveless, ribbed undershirt.

"And we—and we—" Lita's panic made her breathless. "We—we
in a Cadillac. A Cadillac!"

"What?"

"Oh, Jesus, Father God, Lord, help me, Holy Ghost, put shelter
over—"

"Woman, what done turned in you?"

Lita stretched her arms out over the dashboard and began her
prayer again, louder this time.

"Quiet now," Cooley snapped. "If the devil don't wake them, you
will." He grabbed Lita's arm. "Stop that."

Lita pulled away and started again. "Jesus, Father God, Lord—"

"Stop that!" Cooley grabbed her again and tried to pull her down but she squirmed and found her strength, and pushed him off with the power of a man.

"The Word of God is upon me," she said. "You can't harm me!"

Cooley's head bounced off the window and he tasted something salty in his mouth.

"Bitch!"

He slapped her. She slapped back and fought him in the front seat of that Cadillac. There was a tap at Cooley's window. They froze and looked at each other before quickly straightening themselves and sliding into their seats. The window screeched as Cooley rolled it down slowly. A light shined brightly into his eyes.

"Who is this? Oh, boy. Oh, boy! What's a Black motherfucker like you doing here at this rest stop?"

Neither Lita nor Cooley could see anything beyond the blinding flashlight that beamed into the car, as they sat with their hands up. The flashlight was replaced with the muzzle of a pistol. The same voice, nasal and Southern, directed, "Y'all get out that goddamn car."

There'd been lots of "Yes, sirs" and "No, sirs" by the time Lita and Cooley were lined up on the side of the Cadillac. Now they could see the uniform, the badge, the golden buckles, the red-pitted face.

"Yes, sir, officer sir," Cooley was saying. "I'm here going to Chicago and I'm getting married. Me and my girlfriend have found Jesus and we were sitting here praying and I was asking her to marry me."

The red-faced man looked at the car. "You riding mighty fine for a nigger."

"Yes, sir. I'm just doing what I'm told and taking this car that's in my name up to Chicago. I'm probably going to have to sell it so we'll have a place to stay. I had a stroke of luck at one time. I was an athlete in the black league. You know what niggers play." Cooley was talking fast and looking out over the road past the officer's ear. There was no way out. The sleeping heads were starting to move.

"The old White man that I worked for, a good Christian man, who owned the team and the players, he decided that I was good enough to have his old car. And an old nigger like me, I decided that after paying for it for a year and a half that I could drive to Chicago. I decided I was getting married and here in this car, I just proposed to my girlfriend." He was smiling and grinning, waiting for the officer to do the same.

"I got the ring even." He pointed to the car and inched to the door. "Right in the back seat." He reached inside with the curious officer and his pistol tight on his back and produced the ring from the lining of his hat. He handed it to Lita. She slid it on her finger.

"You know, you ain't welcome here," the officer said, not smiling a bit. "You need to drive fast and get out of my rest stop. Ain't no place to rest, for you, until you get to Chicago. And I'm here to tell you, boy, if you're lying about marrying this girl, you're going to run across me again in the highway of life. I may not have the same uniform on, but I swear to God that I will shoot you in the back of your head and say that you tried to fight me or that you raped the same woman that you say you love."

Lita looked at Cooley. She could've been mad. She'd told him to leave. Could've been angry. But she was just scared. And really, she felt closer to Cooley right then. Their hearts were beating this rhythmic melody that only they shared for miles around. They'd leave together. Or die together.

"A promise made is a promise kept. You hear me, nigger?"

"Yes," Cooley said.

"I'm the executioner," the officer said proudly, noticing the growing crowd. "You know what that means?"

Cooley shook his head.

"I will execute as promised to make a big thinking nigger like you, just as dead as any other nigger that I have ever shot along here. And since I'm sheriff and I have been sheriff here a long time, it has been a lot of Black motherfuckers like you who I have shot in the back of the head and they mamas thanked me, for they was no good driving a fast car, talking fast and just wrecking the world."

He looked at the Cadillac again. "It's good niggers and it's bad niggers and I want to know right now is you a good nigger or a bad nigger?"

He turned his flashlight to Lita. She squinted a bit and wiped a tear from her cheek. "Ma'am, is he going to marry you? Will he live with you forever? Cause if he's a good nigger, then I'm going to let him pass. Answer wisely. His life right now is in your hands. So if God and you agree that he should die at this moment, take your time and say, 'pull-the-trigger-on-this-nigger.'"

"No, no, no," Lita said. She could see a woman holding a baby standing off behind the officer. "He's good. He's gonna marry me."

"Well, that's wonderful." The officer finally smiled. "You know what," he started, straightening his shirt, "since you offered me truth, I'm gonna offer you justice. I'm also the Justice of the Peace in this town. Y'all stand up straight now and instead of being the angel of death, I'm going to be God's servant, for I'm a deacon at the church, at Southern Baptist Christian Church." He put the gun back in his holster and pulled a little blue bible out of his back pocket. "I can marry you right here, right now if you so elect, ma'am?"

Cooley and Lita straightened and cupped hands. The crowd gathered behind the officer came in closer.

"Now, do you take this man to be your husband forever?"

"Yes."

"And you, boy?"

Cooley stared at the gun in the officer's holster.

"Say yes, boy."

"Bernie, say yes," Lita pleaded, her hand shaking so wildly, Cooley had to hold it tighter.

"Yes."

The sun was rising over the rest stop as some words were read from some random place in the blue Bible.

"Y'all are now married," the officer soon announced.

The crowd clapped.

"Now you make sure you go on and send for that marriage certificate when you get to Chicago, and don't you dare think of stopping until you get there, or you'll come upon another executioner, just like me. I'm your witness and God saw everything."

"Yes, sir," Cooley said.

"Whoever and whatever you thought you was in this car before I came is dead now. This woman is the only thing next to God that saved you. You's at her mercy. You's married now."

— The Bishop's Radio Address

I remember rolling that window down when I heard the knock. Remembering that pink man and his red eyes stabbing that Caddy and me so many times I was sure the first lady and I wasn't ever gonna make it out of there with our feet flat on the ground? I asked myself, 'Who is this man? Why is his pistol pointed at my temple?' A man doesn't fear another man, but death isn't a prize a hero should be anxious to collect. You hear me out there? I hope you're listening. Because I'm telling how it went. How I died at the rest stop on the border of my past. How my life got changed when I was thinking about turning back.

I won't lie. I had every intention of turning around and driving back into the hell we'd recently left. The first lady was angry Lita then, a woman with the word of Jesus upon her, a woman I'd turned into so many horrible things sometimes I didn't think she'd ever come back. And I, Bernard Cooley, your Bishop Cooley, was Dying Bernie—a pimp who saw his reflection in the mirror and recognized that it was the devil himself. I asked God to help me and then I told Him that He was taking too long. I hope you heard me. I told God He was taking too long. Had my mind made up I was turning around.

But His mind was someplace else. Walking me someplace else. And I remember thinking what kind of God or what kind of spirit would send somebody to make sure I walked the right way? To make sure I got married. Because that's what it was, church. If I ever lacked the faith and belief that God had sent somebody to make sure I was marrying that day and that I was getting ready to be a married man before I got to Chicago, I didn't have to wonder it anymore. There it was. A real man with a real pistol. God's mercy is like that sometimes. Think about that.

But how did I get there? That's what the church wants to know. That's what I told you I'd talk about in today's address. How a pimp and a prostitute, the people you know as Bishop Bernard Cooley and Evangelist Lita Cooley, ended up in a Cadillac at a "Whites only" rest stop on the Georgia-Tennessee border. How God's mercy took one man and made him two. How I got over.

Like most of the men who've shown up at my bible college in the middle of the night with cigarette burns on their hands and stacks of hundred-dollar bills in the trunk, I was born talking my way into things—candy, milk, money, girls, cars. Old folks called me a man when I was very young and while I didn't really quite understand what they meant, I was proud and always kept a few dollars, a story and a hustle in my pocket if I ever needed to prove it. This meant I was smart. And so, school came easy. The streets came easier. And most times, there wasn't much difference between the two.

But as smart as I was, my mother was smarter. She was poor, but she was smart, and I recognized this when I was very, very young. She never went without three or four jobs and she avoided paying taxes by using different people's Social Security numbers who didn't have the smarts to work; so she had to be three and four different people in order to get by. You hear? Three or four.

The only thing that ever made her stupid was my daddy. And, really I guess that actually made him stupid because who she'd become with him would lead her to kill him. Like always, I could hear him beating her. I could see her as she called Jesus and stabbed him in the neck and my uncle came in and helped to call Jesus on him and took the knife out of his neck and smacked him and told him if he ever touched his sister again he'd break his teeth and then his hand went into his mouth. My uncle left. My mother came in with the knife again and that was that. The blood flowed like a river on the living room floor. It came and washed over our toes. I wondered where Jesus was that day. I remember my grandmother throwing a green blanket over my head and praying over me as they took his body out. I remember her saying that my father was going to be a better man in heaven. I remember her saying never to hit a woman like he beat on my mother for so long. That was the smartest thing I'd ever heard.

It seemed like the next day, I was almost a man, and my mother was pushing me out the door to walk up the street to Morehouse College. See, she'd never gone to prison. There wasn't no trial or investigation in those days. A Black man on the floor. A woman saying he fell. That's it. Put him in the ground.

You ain't stupid, and don't you ever be poor," my mother said, as she handed me a napkin holding two pieces of fried chicken when I was leaving for school. 'You come back here with more than this.' I did. I kept the school and the street close, talking my way to graduation from both. And on that day, the streets seemed to have a lot more to offer as far as a position that didn't include working a lot for a little. I'd seen too much of that. My first big gamble got me my first big Cadillac, and that led to my first big job—pimp. It was so easy. Aren't those kinds of things, though for a man like me? A lot of talking and sometimes hitting, but more money than I could hold in my trunk.

Sweet times in a little city that prided itself on keeping a Black man in his place. My money meant I went everywhere. My own mother couldn't argue with the luxury it brought. But luxury in the White man's world gets old for a smart man. I had a brain and my grandmother introduced me to Jesus. And any man knows he can't live in two worlds for too long without going down. Ten years after I began pimping, I was still telling myself I would soon graduate from that lifestyle, but easy money makes it a hard decision.

The night of the dream, I was having a good time. It was one of those weekends that brought silly Negroes in colorful suits with big pockets from all over Florida, Tennessee to Georgia and they all wanted a trick and some gin. I had both—supply and demand.

By the time I found my bed I had three of my own hoes with me and enough cash to get out of the game forever. I thought this. Thought where I'd go. Thought what I'd do. And ain't nothing come. Ain't that something, Church? A smart man with no plan. I closed my eyes thinking I was in heaven already, why leave? A White woman sleeping at my feet, two reds under my arms ... Heaven. Even a saved man would think that. I know y'all are laughing, but it's true.

Well, I went to bed in heaven and woke up in Tupelo. And somewhere in between, I ended up in hell. It was a dream. Depends on how you look at it. I don't know. It was something. I was standing in front of the bathroom mirror and went to look at myself. I saw me, but it wasn't me. What I saw was a dark and peeling mass of fire. Not flames. Anger. Red. In and around me. Like a demon. Me, but changed. My heart stopped. I thought I was dying. I called for those tricks and they didn't answer, so I went to my bed and they were in there touching each other and laughing. Smiling at me. Their faces were distorted. Like men who'd had strokes. But they laughed and fondled each other's breasts. The White one called to me, 'Daddy, you brought me here.'

I didn't know if it was a dream or if it was real. And I don't know that it matters. But I ran. I ran out that house. I ran through the night. I tugged at my face. I felt my chest for my heartbeat. Nothing. I was a crazy man with no soul, seeking himself. And when I didn't find anything, I got in that Cadillac and drove. I drove until I needed gas. And then I drove some more. Went from Atlanta all the way to Tupelo, a place I'd never been, but something told me to stay put. My wheels stopped in front of a little white house with a little Brown girl sitting on the steps looking like she was searching for something. She was Lita, a girl being born into womanhood right there. She was singing about Jesus, and when I got out of the car, she waved. "Come here," she said. I did.

We sat there talking for what was way too long for a man. She unbraided her hair. Said she hated Tupelo. Asked where I'd been. Asked if I could take her there.

"You don't know me."

"I do. You're Bernard Cooley."

"I just told you that an hour ago."

"I know. I was there. I ain't stupid. Ain't no little girl. And I knew you before you pulled up in that."

"A lot of women know me."

"Not like I do." She smiled in this way. "I got to tell you something Bernard Cooley."

"Now I'd seen them demons. I'd seen them in myself and in my bed and now I was talking to an angel. She said she'd spoken to God. And He told her I was coming. Told her to wait for a "BC" to show up on her doorstep.

"I laughed at her. A young girl ain't been nowhere but the church and back and what she know about BC?

"She told me she had a vision of a college. Accredited college that gave doctorates in divinity to men who'd lost their way.

"You lost. Ain't you?"

"I guess so," I answered, looking down at my shoes. See, this girl, maybe ten years younger than me, was seeing right through me. I was ashamed. But I was happy.

"No you found, Bernard Cooley." She got up from where we were sitting on the steps. "Come inside. You got to meet my Memaw when she come home. Got to tell her you taking me to Chicago so we can start this Christian school. And you gonna marry me."

"Chicago? Marry you?"

She didn't even look back at me to respond. I followed her. And later, I told her Memaw, a toothless, chocolate brown woman with grey hair in one long braid, who swore she'd kill me if I was lying, just like Lita had said. We needed to make one stop. Atlanta. I needed some money.

It's funny how a smart man can change what's good to what's bad. Really, that's the business I was in. No man wanted a nasty trick. He wanted the good one. The sweet one. Remind him of the girls in church. That was my calling. Find the good; make them bad. I did this to Lita without thinking. Without trying. I said I needed something and there she was. She believed in me. And so I believed what she believed. I wanted to. I needed to. You understand?

We needed money and whenever we got enough, I said we needed some more. She would cry. Try to write to her Memaw, but then I'd suggest we pray. I'd do whatever to make her stay. At some point, I realized I needed more than her dreams of me. I needed her to be that. And I couldn't lose her. No matter how scared I was.

And that fear is something, ain't it? It made me an angry man sometimes. When she wouldn't listen, I'd think, there she is. She don't believe. She don't believe. She ain't like the rest. She's leaving.

But she didn't leave. On the day I decided to break her, she stood up to me and changed my life. She reminded me of the man she had seen from her porch. She reminded me that Jesus had a plan for me. While I tried to hurt her, curse her and demean her, she got in my car calling the name of Jesus. Set me back on the road to Chicago and that road led me to that rest stop, and that rest stop brought me face-to-face with that White man with the pistol.

It was at that moment that I saw everything she had seen through her prayers. She didn't know that it was a nightmare for me and when she was singing and crying for her life, screaming and calling for Jesus and all that, she was talking to the devil. Who was I? Was I my father? What had I become? Why was I replicating the disturbing truth about my father, the hurt that I felt as he hurt my mother? And here I was hurting someone's daughter. What had come over me? I saw my mother's face in this woman. And all I could hear coming out of her mouth was my mother asking me had I lost my mind. And what in God's name had I become. I was that demon in the mirror. I could see in Lita every woman that I had known in my life who loved and prayed for me. I could hear my mother and my grandmother saying God watched, knew and saw everything we did before we did it.

Well, what did God know that night? What was God doing to me? Lita was in the car and I realized I had to run again. We had to run this time. Run fast to where she said she had to take us. Run to where I knew we had to go.

After facing that White man holding the black steel, I parted ways with my past. It wasn't easy. Death never is. But it's possible that man was sent by God. I'll never change that. While he didn't put a bullet in my heart, he put a bullet in that demon. Lita and I rode right to Chicago with no maps and no stops and when we got here, I sent for those certificates the very next day. She didn't believe it, but I knew I had to. See, it wasn't only a marriage certificate to me. It was a birth certificate. It was how Pimp Bernard Cooley became Bishop Bernard Cooley and if the story was ever to be told, I needed a record of the truth.

Just so you could know. And now you do.

LOVE ME FOREVER

A woman in a tight canary-colored dress exited the passenger side of the old gold-colored Eldorado sitting in the parking lot at the Big Blue Sky Motel.

Hugo was hanging over the rusty railing in front of his grandmother's room on the second floor, watching and listening, waiting for the White man with the fat fingers who was dangling from the open window on the driver's side begging the woman to stay. He held his breath so he could hear even a whimper. The White man with the fat fingers and big car was someone who waited for nothing. But at the Big Blue Sky, a long, glossy red fingernail placed over his lips and the woman in canary whispering, "Esperas" (you wait), had him panting.

Her name was Carmen. She was with Hugo and his grandmother when they came from Cuba ten years ago. Back then, Hugo was an olive-colored baby in his grandmother's arms. So now, no matter how hard he tried, he couldn't remember Carmen in his nightmares about the wet boat. Still, he didn't believe what his grandmother and the other women said about her as they ironed customers clothes in their motel rooms.

The White man leaned over the steering wheel and craned his neck toward Carmen, like a pouting puppy, but it was too late. She was closing the gold door with one hand and straightening her dress with the other.

"Tomorrow?" He queried, flashing a smile that showed all of his teeth. Hugo couldn't tell if this was a question or a plea. Either way, it went unanswered. Carmen tossed a beaded wooden purse over her shoulder and turned her back. She wasn't a small woman so she didn't need to saunter to make everyone around watch her walk away.

The man would sit in his car and wait awhile. They all did. The important men with big cars waited for nothing.

Hugo ran to meet Carmen on the staircase.

Living in America, his grandmother was a maid. She rode two buses to work and on most weeknights had to stay late to make sure everything was in place for Peter and Jane get to school on time. The other women at the motel instinctively looked after Hugo when she was away—made sure the skinny boy wasn't too hungry, washed his face before school and stayed out of the streets. He was a little brother, a nephew, a son, so at every door and at every turn there was an offering of rice and some soft voice saying, "Negro guapo," (handsome black) as he passed. They'd pull him, run their fingers through his coal-colored hair like it was summer grass and say again, "negro guapo." This was how Hugo learned that he was special. Black skin. Jet black hair. They told him that he was their Cuba in Miami.

When Hugo found Carmen, she was halfway up the stairs.

The White man started honking his horn. "Tomorrow!" He yelled. "Tomorrow, Carmen La Vista, you will love me!" He laughed like a madman. "Tomorrow!"

"Hola, Hugo! Guapo, negro inteligente," (Hello Hugo. Handsome, smart black) Carmen said to the lanky boy rushing down to meet her. She rolled her eyes at the honking and handed Hugo the key to her room. "Te pertenezco. Es mi vida. Te amo. Te adora. (I belong to you. It is my life. I love you. I adore you.)

This was a lot for the comprehension of an eleven-year-old boy on a motel staircase—even in a romantic language that rolled off of the tongue and twisted one meaning three ways. A grown woman shouldn't say she belonged to a boy. Shouldn't say he is her life. Shouldn't say she loved him and ask if he loved her back.

Hugo knew to be happy, while his grandmother was still at work and couldn't hear. He'd been told not to speak to Carmen Arnaz, the woman who came with him on the boat from Cuba when he was a baby. He didn't remember her from the journey.

His grandmother said, "Do not look at her. She is a nasty woman. Dirty. Won't work or eat rice like the others."

"Dígame, Hugo. Dígame que usted me adora," Carmen said. "Tell me, Hugo. Tell me you love me…"

"Te amo," Hugo boomed, poking out his chest and fighting to make his still squeaky voice sound tougher than the horn downstairs.

Carmen laughed. She was sweating and reeked the scent of a mango —not sweet, but earthy. She took off her shoes and slowly handed them to Hugo before following him the rest of the way to her room.

Hugo never went inside. His job was to open her door and wait outside until the man downstairs left. Sometimes there'd be flowers or small bottles of perfume wrapped in newspaper left in the doorway. He'd pick them up and hand them to her. She'd give him two quarters for his company. She'd touch his hair and tell him to get back to his room before one of the talking women saw him.

Sometimes, and this was almost never, Carmen allowed one of the men to come upstairs. They'd laugh and rub their fat, pink pig bellies. Next, they'd wink at Hugo standing near the rusty rail and ask how he'd come to know such a full-grown woman. Their breath smelled like tobacco and cheap American beer. Hugo stared at them but never smiled.

There were no presents or flowers waiting in the doorway the day the man in the Eldorado sat outside and honked his horn for ten minutes. Carmen gave Hugo a crisp dollar bill and curled a stray lock, placing it behind his ear with the same finger she'd placed on the white man's lips.

"When I ask you Hugo always answer me you love me forever. I am more older than you," she said in her broken English, "but forever I want your love. Forever when you see me, you tell all the other women that you love me forever. No matter what Hugo promise me."

The eleven-year-old's promise got him his first kiss on the cheek. Carmen took her shoes and left him in the hallway.

As Hugo's voice changed to baritone, his grandmother found work in a home too far for a bus ride so they moved out of the Big Blue Sky Motel. All the women were happy. They had a party in the laundry room. Red streamers and blue balloons were everywhere. They fed Hugo birthday cake with their hands and told him he was lucky and he should never come back. He could go to a good school where the teachers spoke real English. Get a scholarship. He could be a doctor. Not just be a Cuban who came over on a wet boat in a nightmare. Didn't he want that? Should he want that?

He wanted to say goodbye to Carmen Arnaz, but she hadn't been invited to the party.

On weekends, and whenever school released early, Hugo found his way back to see her. Her old canary-colored dress was too tight now and faded to dusty yellow. Her fingernails were cut short and her sweat smelled like his. When he spoke, she'd act surprised. Ask if he still loved her. "Te amo," he'd say humbly, his head bowed and begging for a pet. She'd laugh.

He wished for Carmen's laugh the day he came home from school and found his grandmother in her favorite chair, sleeping but too quiet. He held his breath so he could hear her breathing. There was only quiet. She died in her chair. Her last breath was in America, with her grandson attending a good school. He had a chance at a better life and that was the very reason she came to this country. There was no laughter, not Carmen's, not anyone who knew and loved his grandmother.

Weeks after his grandmother died, a girl Hugo met at school and kissed on the lips asked where his mother was and why she'd let him come to America alone.

"I wasn't alone," he said. "And she didn't want to come. She loves Cuba."

"More than you? That isn't a mother. You don't have a mother."

The next day, Hugo was sitting outside of Carmen's room. He had a bag of mangoes in one hand. A new dress wrapped in golden foil in the other.

"You are a man now," she said. "And I am an old woman. You keep coming back to me." She handed him her key.

He unlocked the door.

"How did we get here?" Hugo asked in Spanish. He was standing in the hallway.

Carmen was in the room. She walked to the bed to take off her shoes. She didn't bother turning on the light. It was summer and the air conditioner hadn't worked in three years.

"You," she answered. "You were in Maela's arms. Smiling. Smiling like we weren't drowning in that sea. The water was in the boat. Splashing in over our feet. But we didn't look down. We all watched you. We all knew you were an angel. A beautiful Black angel. If you loved us, we'd live, forever."

"I don't want to go back to the college," Hugo said. "I want to stay here with you."

Carmen held out her hand and the grown man walked into her room. "I have something for you," she said. She reached under the bed and pulled out a shoebox.

"What is this?" he asked.

"These are all my dreams. I have saved them for you, negro guapo, so you can be a doctor who doesn't eat plain rice or stay somewhere you're meant to leave."

She made him promise not to open it until he got back to school. He didn't wait, though. On the bus back to school, he lifted the frayed edges of the lid and saw a treasure, stacks of hundred-dollar bills.

Carmen was the only person Hugo thought to invite to his graduation. She showed up with grey hair and a young man on her arm. He wasn't as young as Hugo, but he wasn't old enough for Carmen. And Hugo's heart felt sad for thinking this—that any man other than him could be "for" Carmen forever. He smiled at the young man, shook his hand anyway and invited them to a reception at his fraternity house.

Holding a second glass of white wine in her hand, Carmen said, "Hugo, Antonio, he is from Cuba. He now is famous at the museums for his sculptures of anatomy. He studied under the masters."

This was the most Carmen said of any man other than Hugo. The man kissed her hand and asked Hugo too many questions.

"Why did you bring him here?" Hugo asked Carmen after pulling her from the Cuban sculptor's arm.

"You invited me, mi corazón."

"I invited you because I love you. Te amo, Carmen Arnaz," Hugo said. "Tell him that you love me forever."

Carmen was laughing and shaking her grey hair.

"You are confused, my angel, my poor angel," she said, taking Hugo's hands into her own. "God bless you for your love, but there are so many ways to love me forever."

Hugo pulled away. He would not beg her. He would not pant or pout for her love like the other men.

"I brought him here for you," Carmen said to his back. "He will teach you. He will teach you how to wield the scalpel with skill and with elegance. You still want to be a physician don't you? This is my gift to you. He is my gift to you. You will be more than a Cuban angel from the wet boat."

"You are a dirty woman," Hugo spat, turning back to look at Carmen. "A nasty woman who works on her back!"

And then, so fast, Carmen struck the cheek she was first to kiss. She threw the wine in Hugo's eyes and he couldn't see her walk away.

Hugo accepted her gift and learned anatomy from Antonio Ruiz. He went to medical school and became a doctor. He married a woman who never wore canary-colored dresses and knew not to ask of his mother or Cuba.

When he got the news about Carmen Arnaz's broken heart, he was sitting on the deck of his second yacht, "Eldorado," eating slow-roasted pork belly and drinking American beer.

"Carmen is dying," he said to his wife.

"Who is Carmen?" she asked.

"My mother."

The wife had the maid pack Hugo a bag. He was going to stay at the hospital. He was going to fix Carmen's heart.

"I love you," his wife called to him when he walked out the door.

At the hospital, he found Carmen asleep. Her hair was as white as lightning. Her teeth were gone. The doctors said she hadn't been coherent in days. They handed him her chart, but said it was smarter to pray for a dying woman.

Hugo placed his hand over Carmen's heart and her eyes burst open like the sun rolling over the tip of a mountaintop.

"Hugo, tell me you love—" she tried but he placed a finger over her lips.

"Te amo, la madre," he said. "Te amo. You are the light of my heart. My family, my mother, my everything."

Tears rolled down her face and the silence filled the room.

He leaned down and kissed her cheek.

"Tú eres mi corazón," Carmen said. "You are my heart. You are my son. You are my life."

He felt her heart beating slower beneath his palm. There was a long beep. A nurse ran into the room Carmen floated toward the big blue sky, saw her olive baby in another woman's arms and she knew she was loved forever.

INVISIBLE KEYS TO FOREVER

Sometimes, right in the middle of everything that's happening, one small thing—an old red bead rolling across a white linoleum floor, two girls jumping rope in the street, the sound of a car alarm blaring like a screaming baby—can flood the mind with memories of the past that demand we replay them again.

This was happening to Terrance. It was just like any day: the alarm went off, he got into the shower and his brother Keyshawn was in the kitchen cooking scrambled eggs.

Once they got in the car, Keyshawn turned on his iPod, and Terrance pulled out of the driveway to head to work. But then something in that typical day changed. Terrance had been thinking about getting away. Seeing something new. He turned to Keyshawn. His little brother was bobbing his head to something on the iPod.

"You wanna go on a vacation? I was thinking somewhere like the Dominican Republic or maybe Miami or New York. Where would you like to go?" Terrance asked.

Keyshawn was ten years younger than Terrance. He recently graduated from college. He didn't mind working to help Terrance pay the bills. It was the only way their mother would let the little brother move in with the big brother—he had to pay his own way.

Keyshawn kept bobbing his head.

"Nowhere with you. You're always tryin' to get somebody to do what you wanna do and the person who wants to do what you wanna do, you need to be inviting her," Keyshawn responded.

The word "her" was weighty like a rock tossed into a sidewalk pond causing ripples in his mind. Terrance felt the thought vibrate through him, but stopped it somewhere. He turned off the iPod. "But this will be something special. Something different." Keyshawn frowned in a way that reminded Terrance of how young he really was.

"Hangin' with you ain't special," Keyshawn said. "We hang every day when we ride in." Keyshawn turned the iPod back on quite nonchalantly, sat back and closed his eyes.

The ride in was forty-five minutes in a parade of traffic that moved slowly for no reason. It took them from a maze of starter homes that once belonged to new families—a husband with a hard-hat, a fairly pretty pregnant wife and a small furry puppy—to what Atlanta claimed was downtown but was more like a pretend city with planned promenades and more vacancies than dwellers. There, they'd leave the car in a parking deck and pad through the empty streets to be at their desks by 6:30 am.

Terrance had been a day trader for a little over two years. He impressed his boss with his ability to work out complex figures right in his head. He could come think up an analysis in a few minutes, something that would take another trader hours on a laptop. When Keyshawn graduated and didn't even look for a job, Terrance walked into his boss's office and said something like, "If you think I'm good with numbers, wait until you meet my brother." Long dreadlocks with blond tips, a tattoo on his left wrist, Keyshawn didn't look the part like Terrance did, but he had double the talent. Trading came easy to him. When he started, he became a company marvel. The boss put Keyshawn's desk right next to Terrance.

"Bruh, you's about to be thirty," Keyshawn said with his head still relaxed, his eyes closed. "Or are you thirty-two? I'm twenty-two, so yes, you's thirty-two. Yo!"

"You's? Yo! " Terrance mocked his brother and looked at the tie around his neck in the rearview mirror.

"Who gives a shit? I'm in the car with you. You missed the point too, Einstein."

"Which is?"

Keyshawn opened his eyes.

"You talk to me like we gon' do a vacation together, just us, but you know I know I ain't the person you want to be with on no vacation. I ain't the person you should be with on no vacation," he repeated. "And I don't want to go on a vacation with you. I like babes. You like brie. It's all good, bruh."

The brothers laughed. Just like that, everything was known. They were a decade apart in age, but had always been very close. Terrance's father left before he could walk. And Keyshawn's father was a better man, a preacher, but he died before Keyshawn could walk. Terrance played father. He was always proud of his little brother. He taught him to walk while their mother was out working two jobs. He planned everything in his life to include his brother. Nothing could be planned without him. Sometimes, Terrance thought that was why pebble-she left in the middle of the night.

"What the fuck is brie anyway?" Keyshawn was still laughing. Terrance had pulled back to a fading chuckle. "Where you get that shit from? Her?"

And then there was another reference to "HER", placed in the air as easy as a rock is tossed into a sidewalk pond. After a quick mental sidetrack, Terrance started again with the vacation topic.

"What about New York? We could visit the Big Apple. I've been thinking about getting us transferred there."

Keyshawn closed his eyes.

There were chrome handles on the tall glass doors leading into Schwartz Financial. They were big and beautiful. They were so spectacular people would stop and look at them, comment on how they shined like mirrors, reflecting round faces back to you like the Cloud Gate, the Big Bean in Chicago. And they did. They should've. At Mr. Schwartz's demand, these handles were shined every day before anyone touched them to walk into the office. He'd gotten them during one of his many travels abroad to some exclusive place anyone who was employed at Schwartz Financial would likely never see. He said they should remind everyone each day of their potential.

Where they could go if they really put their minds to it.

Terrance was holding onto one of these chrome handles, letting his brother walk into the office before him when he saw two Black men get off the elevator, make a left, and come up behind Keyshawn. The two were tall. Both over six feet tall. Dressed in black. One in a hooded sweatshirt with a black baseball cap.

Keyshawn saw his brother looking behind him, so he also stopped and turned. He removed his ear buds and poked out his chest slightly in a way that only the two other brothers could read. There was one firm on the sixth floor. Keyshawn and Terrance were the only Black men who worked there.

The men were quiet. They came up closer behind Terrance and Keyshawn. The music from the iPod in Keyshawn's hand flooded the space between them. It was dark outside.

"Can I help you?" Terrance asked, his voice pleasant but strong, a mix of College Park, Georgia and two degrees from Emory University.

"This Schwartz?" The one in the hooded sweatshirt asked. He was younger than the other one.

"Yes."

"We meeting with Schwartz."

"Mr. Schwartz? You're meeting with Mr. Schwartz?" Terrance asked. He could hear the surprise in his voice and hated himself for it. Schwartz only met personally with the firm's wealthiest clients. Suddenly, he noticed the black diamond Rolex on the younger man's wrist. "He doesn't come in until seven."

They all stood there. All four. Toe to toe. Terrance's hand was still on the shiny chrome handles.

"You can wait in the lobby." The strength left his voice. "We can't…we can't…we're not allowed to let anyone in the office before we open. What time did he say he was meeting—"

"Hey!" A voice came from inside the glass doors too cheerful for a morning with no shining sun. "There you guys go!"

Terrance and Keyshawn turned to see Mr. Schwartz walking toward them. His long, stringy hair combed over from one side of the shiny bald spot on his head.

He extended his hand past Terrance holding the door and

beckoned for the men in black to come inside.

"Thanks for coming in so early. I find it's best to get these decisions made early in the day before the market opens." He went on as the men passed the brothers. "Good Morning Terrance, Keyshawn," he addressed them more as an afterthought, as he directed the men in black to his office.

That abrupt pleasantry dominated much of Terrance and Keyshawn's conversation in their cubicle throughout the morning. While standing at the coffee maker, Terrance learned the men owned a strip club. They'd met Schwartz at their business and explained why they wanted to come to his.

By the time the market opened and the men in black were gone, Terrance had presented to his team the deal he'd been working on over the weekend. Keyshawn ran the PowerPoint presentation, and watched the room for agreement and dissent.

Joe Bratski was from the West Coast. He had blond hair that reminded everyone of the beach. He'd started at Schwartz with Terrance and usually backed his ideas.

Martin Leibovitz had gone to business school at Emory with Terrance. They'd been friends—what people in the business world called friends—but since Terrance got Keyshawn the job at Schwartz, Martin, who they all called Leibovitz, managed to find something wrong in everything Terrance did.

"Fucking kid comes in here right from college?" Leibovitz once said to Bratski once over a beer. "I worked my ass off in grad school to get here and now Schwartz lets some street kid with nappy hair come in. What the fuck?"

Keyshawn watched Leibovitz write notes like charges during the presentation. He knew everything Leibovitz would ask. Had the answers prepared to back his brother's idea. This was what he hated about business. How personal it could be when everyone kept saying it wasn't. Talent should've been enough. But it never was. You needed papers. Letters behind your name. He hated his degree for that.

When the presentation was completed, Leibovitz started right in with his questions. Keyshawn was ready to defend Terrance's figures, but it became apparent that Terrance needed no back up.

He left the conference room with Schwartz smiling at him and his hand on his back. The deal was done.

After giving each other a quick dap that no one could see, the brothers fell into their chairs inside their cubicle. Terrance sat back like a big man and grinned at the ceiling.

"New York," he said. "That's where we should go. Check things out. Plan. Maybe we could get a place for Mama, too."

"Yeah, right. Mama leave College Park?" Keyshawn rolled his eyes and turned to face his computer to scan emails. He didn't have his own clients yet. He was backing Terrance until Schwartz trusted him with his own list. It wasn't about talent. The young brother still needed some polishing to talk to people.

"Why not?"

"Not everyone wants to leave College Park like you, you know."

"Why not?" Terrance repeated as Leibovitz walked by with his nose in the air.

"Because everyone's real there," Keyshawn said before lowering his voice to whisper. "Not a bunch of fucking fakes."

The phone on Terrance's desk began to shake and clatter. He picked it up to see her name on the screen. Lydia. It was a text. He dropped it again and looked back up at the ceiling.

Keyshawn rolled over and reached for the phone.

"Touch it and you're dead," Terrance said without looking down.

Keyshawn snatched the phone anyway.

"It's either Mama or Lydia." He looked at the screen. "Lydia." He set the phone back on the desk and laughed.

"Whatever."

"Just read it."

"Whatever."

The phone shook and clattered some more. There were three more messages from her.

"Just see what she has to say. Damn."

"She left me. Who cares what she has to say?"

She had in fact left. But only because, according to Lydia, Terrance had left her a long time prior to then. She said he'd been pushing away. Away with work, with his mother, with his brother, with everything. She was ready to get married. To move in. It had been six years since he'd bumped into her cart in the produce section at the supermarket and complained that she didn't have any pork inside. It was time. Then he moved Keyshawn in.

"I don't see what the big deal is," Keyshawn said at his desk. "I like her—"

"You don't know her."

"She's cool. A little stuffy and whatever, but mad cool. Good to you. Likes that shit you like."

Terrance glared at Keyshawn. He'd been telling him to stop cursing in the office. Keyshawn pointed out that everyone else did. "Well, you're not everyone else," Terrance had said. "I'm not everyone else. Get it?"

"Sorry, damn," Keyshawn said. "I mean, sorry." He paused. "Look, man, just read her texts."

The phone shook and clattered again.

"Clearly, she has something to say." Keyshawn paused again. "Stop being a... prick."

Terrance rolled his eyes and reached for the phone. He handed it to Keyshawn and instructed him to read.

"Damn," Keyshawn said after a minute. "She's mad. Really mad."

"What did she say?"

"She loves you."

They looked at each other.

Terrance took his lunch alone. He needed to think. Lydia wanted to get married. He thought about the night she awakened in the middle of the night, rolled over with tears in her eyes and said she was ready. If he moved Keyshawn into the house it was clear to her that he wasn't ready and that they weren't on the same page. She couldn't stop lying to herself. She wanted a husband. A family. A furry puppy. She cried harder at this sentimental exaggeration—she was a writer and had this way of expressing herself. She got out of the bed and put on her clothes in the dark. Terrance didn't stop her. He stayed there and stared at the ceiling. Responding with what he has said all his life, "My brother needs me," over her tears. He warned her not to leave. That if she did, that was it. It was over. She did. Left in the night. Said she was going to start her life now.

Terrance couldn't focus on his food. He threw the barely-eaten sandwich into the garbage. "Invest. Plan. Move. Get my family out." Terrance had memorized these words and said them again in his head as he walked out of the sandwich shop headed nowhere in particular. It was his map. He'd shared it with Lydia one night after two bottles of wine. But she didn't understand. Couldn't. She'd moved to Atlanta from Miami. Her parents were attorneys who'd begged her to use their money to become the writer they couldn't. She didn't eat pork or red meat. Liked brie. African music. Good wine. Loved New York. Loved the subway. These were the reasons he loved her. But they were also the reasons he secretly thought they could never be together.

"Mama," Terrance said into his phone.

"Hey, baby. How you doin'?"

He could hear the fatigue in her voice. Although he made enough to pay half of her bills so she didn't have to work a day job, she was still working at night.

"I'm fine," Terrance said. "You sound tired."

"Just got in. Worked a double."

"A double? Why, Mama?"

"Got bills. We all got bills." She laughed a little. Coughed. She still smoked.

"But I paid the mortgage."

"You brother has student loans," his mother said. "Look, what you calling with all these questions and accusations for anyway? And why weren't you two over for Sunday dinner last night?"

"I had a presentation today at work and—"

"You always got some presentation at work. But you only got one Mama, and when I'm dead and gone—"

"Mama, please!" Terrance groaned at the oft-repeated threat.

"That's okay, though. I didn't sit in this here house alone, anyway. Had me a visitor." Her voice promised gossip.

Terrance took the bait.

"Who?"

"Lydia."

Ripples in the pond. The mother, of course, could sense the ripples through her son's body.

"Hum …," she said in the space of Terrance's cold pause. "Guess that's why you calling. Got Lydia on the brain."

"No it's not." Terrance tried to laugh. "Why was she at the house?" He imagined Lydia sitting on his mother's black leather sofa in her only church dress. She didn't believe in religion, but loved the choir, so she went most Sundays and wore the same dress as an act of defiance.

"Third Sunday. She came to help me water my plants. Same as always. Mighty big of her to come help me after my son dumped her."

"I didn't dump her. She left me," Terrance pleaded like he was arguing over a toy with Keyshawn.

"She wanted to get married, son. She wanted to marry you."

Terrance exhaled like this was news again.

"It was all she was talking about. Why? Everyday."

"And what's wrong with that? That's what she's supposed to do. What, you expect her to just sit around and wait for you forever?"

"You're starting to sound like her."

"Maybe that's because she's right."

Terrance had made it to the front of the job, but stood outside the building where the smokers usually took their breaks.

"She ain't right. I got plans. You know it and she knows it. She doesn't understand me," he said.

"Understand what? You're always trying to put the entire world on your shoulders. I told you to let go of all of that," his mother commanded, her voice rising as she sat upright in her bed. "I told you. You got a good thing with Lydia. She's a jewel. And you know what, that's the thing about fools like you."

"What?"

Terrance was listening. This was what he'd called for, but didn't know it.

"You men never know what you've got until you lose it. You find a treasure and then try to bury it. But you can't bury Lydia. She shines, son. And some other fool is gonna come on by and pick her up as soon as you walk off."

Terrance didn't even like the idea of this. He balled up his fists without thinking.

"That's what I told her, too. Told her not to worry. Someone's gonna come into her life real fast. A good man. Like Keyshawn's daddy. Thank you, Jesus."

"Why would you say something like that to her?"

"Because it's true. You watch." She laughed a wicked laugh, but then sensed the waves around her firstborn's heart and stopped. She paused for clarity and then said, "You know, you can't try to take care of us anymore. Time for you to start your life. Marry that girl."

"She left me, Mama."

"She ain't gone nowhere but up the street somewhere. Waiting for you to say something nice. Call her up. Take her somewhere. Take her to the beach. Talk to her."

"This is Atlanta. There aren't any beaches here," Terrance replied.

"Well, take her someplace nice. Away from here. Your Aunt Sonia's house on the beach in Savannah. A vacation. Yeah. When's the last time you've been on a vacation? You probably ain't even thought of no vacation."

"Actually—"

"You can ask her to marry you there, too. Right at your Aunt Sonia's house on the beach on Tybee Island. Right on vacation. Don't tell her anything. I won't tell her either. Surprise her. She'll love it. Take a camera."

"Slow down, Mama," Terrance said. "I didn't agree to any of this."

"Yes, you did, son. You just did."

"Savannah? Come on. You know how Aunt Sonia is about that place. She'll never let me use it. I'd be better off renting a hotel." Terrance couldn't believe what he was saying, but he kept talking and the more he spoke, the more he believed this was what he was going to do.

"No hotel. It must be at the house. It's how I see it in my mind. There's something about the house. That's why your aunt protects it like that."

"Should I call her up and ask her to use her house for the weekend? Just like that? When I know she's never let anyone else use it before?"

"Don't call her. Go see her. Talk to her. Tell her your plans."

"I don't have any plans. I'm just talking to you," Terrance protested.

"Yes, you do. Yes, you do."

Keyshawn was still eating a sandwich at his desk when Terrance got back. He sat down at his desk and turned to his little brother.

"Hey, what would you do if I moved to New York without you?" He asked.

"Yo, all morning you begging me to go on vacation with you. And now you come back to your desk and talk about leaving? Mad schizophrenic!" Keyshawn rose from his seat and picked up his laptop.

"Seriously. Would you be cool if I left?"

Keyshawn frowned. "Yes! I got me. You got you? I'm on my grown man 'ish.' "

Keyshawn started walking away.

"Where are you going?"

"Schwartz. He came when you were at lunch. Wants me to handle the portfolio for the brothers from the strip club."

"Really?" The smile on Terrance's face was instant.

"My grown man 'ish!' " Keyshawn popped his collar and walked off.

His mother was right. Getting Lydia to the beach house in Savannah wouldn't be too hard. He'd have to sweet talk her. He'd show up at the coffee shop where she wrote each day with flowers. However, getting access to the beach house would be more difficult. His Aunt Sonia owned the perfect piece of property. And protected it like it was the child she'd never had. Because it was. Unlike her sister, his mother, Sonia had gone to college. She became a poet and then went back to college twice to get a Ph.D. and support her poetry that no one was buying. She never married or had a child. Instead, she lived in a studio in downtown Atlanta and spent every dime she had on the beach house in Savannah. Though she only went there a few times each year, she said the place gave her enough love to last the weeks apart.

Keyshawn went to the strip club with Schwartz after work, and while Terrance got into the car with the intentions of driving the forty-five minutes home alone, the empty seat next to him made him turn the car around to head back downtown to talk to Aunt Sonia about the beach house.

Terrance could hear his aunt breathing on the other side of the studio door downtown.

Like her sister Barbara, Sonia still smoked and though she was quietly trying to figure out if it was her nephew standing in front of her door, her wheezing had greeted him minutes ago.

"It's me, Aunt Sonia," Terrance said.

"Terrance?"

"Yes."

Sonia looked harder into the peephole.

"Why didn't you call first?"

There'd been these break-ins. Young men forcing themselves into old people's homes with lies. They were all happening in huge homes in the suburbs, but Sonia had been watching the news a lot and promised herself that she'd be more careful. She was teaching poetry at Georgia State University and some kids there had gotten robbed at gunpoint right around the corner.

A series of locks were being undone. Click. Click. And clack. And click again. And then the door opened. Aunt Sonia appeared in the doorway like a little beautiful elf with long braids. She was the shortest person in the family, yet she had the biggest smile.

"Well, I wanted to talk to you about the beach house. About using it... maybe. Like this week—"

"Well, why didn't you say that?"

"I was waiting until I got inside," Terrance said. He hugged his aunt and kissed her on the forehead. She smelled like frankincense and myrrh and had a red dot tattooed between her eyes.

Sonia waited until the pot of ginger tea was boiling before she got back to the beachhouse conversation and asked why Terrance wanted to use it. She wanted a reason to give someone the keys. But no reason seemed reason enough. The last request came from Keyshawn. He wanted to have some friends at the house during spring break. She'd said "No."

Terrance told his aunt everything about Lydia. About her crying. The puppy. Leaving in the middle of the night. His life plans.

"Life is a challenging journey," Aunt Sonia said, pouring Terrance a second cup of ginger tea.

"What do you mean?"

"You never know exactly where it's going to take you. But there will be sunrises and there will be storms. There will be moments where life seems so cold that it's downright numbing. And humans get to experience it all. But now it looks as though you have something on your heart." She turned from the table and walked the kettle back to the stove. "You know your heart speaks even when you can't think. The hearts speaks when you don't know what to do, and God speaks through the heart."

"But, how do you follow what your heart says when your mind says something else?" Terrance asked.

"When your mind tells you to listen to your heart," Aunt Sonia said. "Does your heart want to marry this girl?"

"I think so." Terrance's voice was sober. The ginger seemed to open him up, warming his spirit.

"Well, now you have to have the mind to follow your heart." Aunt Sonia slid a single key from underneath a napkin on the table. "This is the key to the house."

"Really?" Terrance tried not to smile. "You're going to let me use it?"

Sonia nodded.

"Wait...you already had it out? But why? You didn't even know I was coming."

"Your mama called boy. Told me everything. I couldn't say no to my baby sister."

"I don't know, Aunt Sonia. She's so sure about Lydia. But I'm not so sure...about myself," Terrance realized.

Sonia folded Terrance's fist over the key in the palm of his hand.

"You take her to the beachhouse and you will know," she said. "You look into her eyes. Read one of the many poems I've written on walls in the house to her. They spoke to me and I wrote what they said. They said new love was coming to our family. The walls said it was time for two to join hands in God's and take the covenant of being man and wife. And the house told me it would begin there."

Her voice was nearly a whisper. Terrance couldn't hear or couldn't believe half of what she was saying, but he didn't dare question her wisdom. He took the key, finished his tea, and stood up knowing he was more of a man leaving his aunt's house than he'd been when he'd gotten there. Before he left with a plan to call Lydia from the car, Aunt Sonia asked him to read aloud one of her poems:

It will not add up.
There is no way to make an acquisition of a heart
That does not long or want to be held.
There's no look for love that is permanent.
For there is no material that should captivate the heart
Or the eyes the way the spirit does in love.
And with each day that mothers love their children
Love loves those who love it back.
But it does not guarantee
There is a place in my heart that I want filled.
There is a dream that I want to walk through life with
That person whose invisible hand will meet mine and I will know.
That upon finding that person I will grow
We will grow from two to three or four.
But we will remember that we entered
Through love's door.

Terrance showed up at the coffee shop with his flowers the next day and offered Lydia his heart. He wanted to take her away. To go to his Aunt's beachhouse so they could talk.

Lydia put up more of a fight than he'd thought, but in the end, her eyes softened as she gazed at the man she loved and she said, "Yes." On one condition: they were going to the beachhouse as friends. No wine. No brie. And no sex. They were going to talk. Terrance agreed and laughed at Lydia's reach for chastity. It was an unexpected request. That was another reason he loved her.

When he picked her up the next week to go to Savannah, right on top of an open bag she'd handed him to carry to the car, there was a bottle of wine and a wheel of brie.

INSIDE OF YOU

Every day, as I open the door to my shop, I think of what I must look like to you. The sun is finally pushing its way through the clouds from the night before. You're sitting in your normal spot at the edge of the bench beneath the sign for the bus stop out front and I'm nervously fumbling with silver-coated keys. I'm wearing the same reliable sweater, the same pea green pleated corduroy pants, and the same brown shoes as every yesterday. I wonder. Do you see me like this? Can you ever see me?

I see you. Your perfect hair. A different coat for every day of the week. High heels—no scuffs. Sunglasses ready for the promise of sun.

I wonder if you'll ever find the thing you're digging for inside that huge designer bag you carry. I pray that you don't know the time and ask me. My watch is on my wrist and I checked before I left the car—just in case.

I hope you miss your bus one morning. You need help and rush into my shop. And who knows. Maybe you like green pants and out-of-shape sweaters. A man who's too young to look so old. I'm what you've been waiting for. You kiss me and we run away to Fiji… and then Guadalajara…Eritrea. I'm wearing shorts. No thick black glasses. Maybe sunglasses.

But, of course, the bus comes. You find the tiny thing in your purse. You get up and disappear until tomorrow's rising sun.

And looking from the other side of my shop window, I wonder, does she see me like this?

Once your bus rolls away, the days in the shop are long and quiet. Even the phone ringing, the daily tapping sound from the adopted three-legged Calico flicking its tail against the window fades to silence. For ten years, I've bought and sold beautiful things in this square box. I was a small-time painter with big dreams. After getting my Ph.D. in Art History from NYU, it was my dream to open an African art store in downtown Brooklyn. Bring the work to the people. Bring my work to the people. I spent time, tirelessly, fighting these Black people to see what I see in this work, in my work, until one day I realized the shop was all and everything I had. It was okay when at twenty-five and fresh out of graduate school, fearless and naïve enough to believe I had the skill to put out on canvas the very characteristics of our people and they would buy it. But ten years later and I'm doing portraits, and selling more Ashanti stools and masks than my own paintings of "inside sunsets," wondering if there will ever be anything else.

Brooklyn has changed, though. When I got here, there were no women like you sitting at the bus stop. No designer bags or people who had a different coat for every day. They come in now, look around. Buy some items and ask about others. And I think, maybe if this place and these people can change, I can as well. I hope. But I am frozen by this place like the eyes in the iconic portraits. I don't bother to try to make them move. This gift of seeing inside of someone and not being inside of someone is what keeps me from moving. I'm smart. I'm definitely lonely. But a drowning man can't stop the tide from turning. So, I say to myself I should be happy to have this place, if nothing else. My friends had other dreams, money dreams, and other clothes, expensive clothes they wore while disappearing into drugs and lies. They learned that art is promised to no man at the altar and though they lived with a little of everything I never had, they died with nothing. I'm lucky. Right? I'm frozen. Right?

"You need someone," the wife of a devoted customer who's bought more of my paintings than he should, said, picking a lint ball from my sweater. "A wife. A girlfriend. Someone to fix you up."

"Oh, Gwendolyn," the man at her side said, feigning embarrassment at her pushiness. "You mind your business. Marcial is an artist. He has no time to think of women...or the lint balls on his sweater."

"It's fine," I said.

I looked down at my sweater to see the wife was still picking away and sucking her teeth. She was wearing pearls. Real pearls—they're a different kind of white—and a fur coat.

"Anyway, Marcial," the man went on, "We didn't come here to cross-examine you about your love life. We came because I want to give my wife a special treat."

"A treat?" The woman let go of my sweater and turned to her husband. "What treat? What's the treat, Walter?" She smiled and her eyes were as clear as the pearls around her neck.

Walter is an investment banker with two offices: one in Queens, another in Bed-Stuy. He typically walks around downtown like it's always spring and knows everything right to say. As he stood there beside his wife, he shook his keys in his pocket and grinned.

"Tell me," his wife demanded, sliding her arm around his fat waist like a daughter hugging her father. I saw her brown fingers sneak beneath the clasp of his belt.

"I'm going to immortalize you, my dear," he said before kissing her on the nose. "Well, Marcial here is going to immortalize you." He slid three pictures of her from his pocket and handed them to me.

In the first one, her hair is pulled back from her face. She's smiling and the glints of light from a single flame on a cake in front of her push into her muddy irises.

"That's from our one-year anniversary," Walter said, pointing at the cake over my shoulder. "Ten years ago and she hasn't aged a bit." He looked at her.

In the second, she's pregnant and her skin is as smooth and tight as the outside of a sweet melon. One hand is beneath her stomach and the other is blowing a kiss at the picture taker.

"Five years after we got married, we had our first child, Tabitha."

Walter pulled his wife into his arms and we stood there in a line. The third was all white. The light in the background was static and harsh. It spilled into Gwendolyn's nude face like the rays of sunlight you see from an airplane window and though it was so close I could see little else, I could tell she was on a beach, reclining on a chair and looking over at Walter beside her. Grains of sand dusted her shoulder. Every mark on her face was defined.

"Fiji," she said, leaning on my hand that held her expressionless image. "That was last month."

"It was our last day on the beach," Walter added tenderly as if I wasn't standing there. "You said you could stay there forever."

"I wanted to," she purred.

I could feel them locking hands beside me. Their warmth almost fell into me. And I would've moved, but the picture wouldn't let me.

Accidentally, two photos fell from my hand and neither of them bent to retrieve them.

I watched. I looked into the whiteness around Gwendolyn, how it demanded so much from her face to simply exist in the overexposed photo. The way a painter sees images, sees light, this was almost death, a murder of the focus. But somehow there was this life I saw in Gwendolyn's eyes that hadn't existed in the other photos, not even in her standing right in front of me. The image was honest and open. And without ever seeing or speaking to Gwendolyn again after that first day of our meeting and seeing that image, I'd know she was a woman full of life. Transparent and content. She owned passion and desire in her eyes. Owned it.

"Can you do something with this?" Walter asked and I realized I hadn't looked up from the image, though they'd now retrieved the other photos on the floor and were now looking at me.

"Yes," I said and it was soft, but I hadn't meant it that way.

Gwendolyn was looking at me. Learning and knowing something in the silent way women do that made Walter and I uncomfortable.

I looked down at the picture.

"So how long will it take?" Walter went on, slicing into the silence. "And money is no issue. You name the price. I know you're worth it.

I know you can capture —"

"Give me that picture." Gwendolyn interrupted Walter. Her voice was grave and direct.

I didn't look up but I could see her hand pushed out toward me.

"What?" Walter asked.

"Give it to me," she insisted this time.

I looked at her, but before I could hand it over, she snatched it and slid it into her purse.

"Gwendolyn, what in God's name are you doing?"

She apologized and slid her hands into mine.

"I want you to find someone that's in your life who is beautiful and who you see coming into your mind each and every day," she said. "I am in my husband's life and he can see me in his mind each and every day. And the way he sees me, no other man should. No other man should have to look into my eyes the way he does, to know me, to see me. He should have his own woman to see into that way...to know in that way."

"Jeez, Gwendolyn." Walter chuckled. "You act like the man is painting a nude picture of you! He's an artist. He's knows what he's doing."

Gwendolyn stared at me. "I love my husband. And I know how he looks at me, how he undresses me with his eyes," she said to me as if Walter hadn't said a thing. "You have to know the same thing and if you do, you know why I can't let you do this."

There was quiet. The Calico hobbled by, weaving slowly between our legs.

"You understand?" Gwendolyn asked.

I was frozen.

She stomped and cursed.

"Gwennie—" Walter tried, but then seeming like she had to move to express something, she grabbed at him and forced a kiss upon his lips that was desperate, so passionate that his body trembled and relaxed.

I thought it would end quickly, but it didn't actually. She cupped his face. He linked his hands beneath her buttocks. They stumbled toward a table and knocked a stack of hand-painted greeting cards over. He picked her up and laid her out. And I, needing anywhere to hide my thoughts picked up my sketchpad, my pencil, and began to copy. As they moved, I moved. I traced the lines of the image before me, emptied what I knew about both of them onto that pad and when they rested, a mound of human lust on my table, I retired to my chair in the corner and stroked the cat.

"I'll give you ten thousand dollars and upon delivery, I'll pay another ten," Walter said when it was done.

Gwendolyn was quiet. She put her fur back on, straightened her hair and fingered her pearls in silence until they left.

Three years later, and our routine was still routine. Walter's twenty thousand dollars was spent on a painting loft and rolling chair for the cat, who'd yet to claim a name. The sun had risen many times on your habit of fumbling through different designer bags and while the smarter me told me to let you go, I never once left my car in the morning without knowing the time.

———

"You should sell gum." I heard this behind me one morning. I was reorganizing a stack of paintbrushes I'd washed.

"Excuse me?" I asked, turning away from the brushes to answer my stranger. My heart tried to kill itself immediately. You were beside me and the wet brushes, holding a new designer bag and smiling. "Gum?" It's the only word I recalled hearing and so I repeated it. You were so close I could see the grey hairs in your ponytail.

"Yeah—for the people waiting for the bus. We could come in and get gum. Maybe even coffee, too." You giggled and smiled a little like you've known me.

"But this is an art store," I said. "And I only sell art." I looked around the store to lead your eyes past the Ashanti stools, masks from around Africa, paintings of Black people, and a corner set of my work, knowing my statement must make perfect sense, but really thinking coffee and gum might not be a bad thing. I could give you what you needed. Maybe you'd stay.

"Can you imagine..." you started, changing the subject and walking around, and I followed. Two steps behind. Still with my heart racing and knowing I must have been looking at you like you were Venus de Milo. From the bench, I could never see your backside. Not bad. Be cool, I told myself.

You stopped at a rain stick from Mexico and studied the carvings of a running man and flames traveling up its spine.

"Seven years I've been sitting on the bench outside and I never once came in," you said matter-of-factly. "I always said I would, but I never did. I was always in a rush. You know?"

"Yes," I agreed, but I was still considering the tense of your statement—was—and I thought of your bus. The sun was up and you were with me. "You missed your bus?" I stuttered. "Why now?"

"Now?" You stopped and spun around like a toddler in a water sprinkler. "Well, I'm free. Today, I'm free."

"Free? You missed your bus?"

"No, I let the bus miss me. I quit my job."

You smiled and I realized you wanted me to say something, but what?

"What happened?" I leaned my head to the side.

"I was sitting out there on that bench and thinking, I'm looking for something and it isn't out here. It's just not...not in my life."

"Well, what are you looking for?"

"Everything. Nothing." You shrugged your shoulders and I heard the Calico's roller bell tolling behind us. "I don't know. I guess I need to look inside of myself and see. I'm Melanie." You switched the ivory purse off your hand and up along your shoulder and extended your hand. Before I realized the automatic gesture, my hand was in yours.

"Marcial."

"So, this is your place, huh?"

"Yes."

"Yeah, I've seen you before. You walk past the bus stop every morning. I always see you."

I looked down at my corduroys to see the Calico standing still beside me in his cart and looking at you. Together we must have looked like an odd army. You reached to pet the cat and asked his name. But I couldn't answer. And for the first time in a long forever I felt the need to demand something and said, "You should've come in. You should've come in sooner."

To this, you replied, "I know."

Over six weeks, I learned everything about you. You liked Chinese food but hated egg rolls. You jumped into the ocean, but couldn't swim. You hated that I noticed how many coats you had, how many purses you carried. You hated how long you stayed at that job. You hated that you didn't know what you would do next. You hated losing at Checkers. You loved dark chocolate and epic films from China. You told me you cooked gourmet versions of soul food and served it with expensive wine. Every detail you shared added color to the painting in my mind.

My need to know you swelled and my subtle demand turned to others. But soon after spending days in the shop searching for a new job on your laptop, you had some questions of your own. You asked why I worked so hard. Why was I alone without someone in my life? Why did I elect to be a retailer, a service provider, when I clearly had the ability to do other things? Other people should sell my art. I should be living the life of an artist. We argued about what that meant.

"Could I watch you work?" You asked one morning after you showed up carrying a box of new clothing you'd bought me with your first severance check. "I've been going into all of the shops on this street," you said. "Do you know there's a tailor two corners down?"

"Emanuel," I answered. "His shirts cost two hundred dollars."

"Well, now you have three."

On a caramel-colored shirt with my initials stitched on the pocket, I painted a blue sunset for you. I said this is how I felt before you appeared in my life like night was frozen around me and there could be no sun. You cried and ran out. I wanted to think you'd never come back, but I knew you would and later that night when I was closing the register and heard the cat's cart wheeling near the front door, I looked up to see you standing there.

"I was a blue sunset, too," you said and I saw that you had no purse on your arm. "That's what was inside of me until you came into my life. But I'm coming alive now."

You pushed your way into the store and your eyes fell into me. I saw your soul—you were learning something new and somehow I knew it was all about me.

"What do you mean?" I asked.

"I mean... I just... I feel like I've been searching for you for a very long time. And I'm so angry that you were right here. Right behind me. Right beside me," you said. "I love you."

"You love—"

You grabbed me and kissed me so desperately, so passionately, my body trembled and then relaxed.

My glasses fell to the floor.

I slid my hands beneath your buttocks and picked you up. I carried you to the table with the stack of hand-painted greeting cards. I laid you out like a painting that I'd sketched in my mind for decades. I entered you and felt my insides become known. My whole self. Your breathing became mine and together we collapsed into ecstasy.

"What do we do now?" I inquired when we finished.

You smiled and sat up on the table. "I was thinking we could go to Eritrea," you said. "You ever think of going to a place like that?"

IF YOU REACH FOR IT

If you saw us on our wedding day, you would never know where we were from. Most everything was dressed in something white. And what wasn't white, was silver. Real silver. Shiny, spectacular silver. Candelabras and special knives made specifically for cutting butter. Everyone there was smiling and talking about where Muriel and I were going, but all I could think about was where we'd been. Roaches on their backs, dead and dried up in the corners in the hallway. Golden pools of piss reeked in the elevator. Muriel crying on the other side of the cinder block wall. Me on my knees praying. Me wanting to help her so badly.

Muriel was a Spelman College graduate who had dreams of opening her own Christian daycare center. She liked working with little people with little hands who were still young enough to name everyone they knew during bedtime prayers. I was on my way to the seminary. I'd gotten accepted to a small school in Kentucky. It wasn't one of the top ten I thought God would send me to, but my mother said I ought to be grateful anyway. She said I had many things to be grateful for. Muriel was one of them. Leaving Harlem was another. I wasn't so sure about that one. Harlem was where I first heard Muriel's heartbeat through the wall in the living room. Harlem was where God first spoke to me. Over screaming women, and screaming men, and screaming babies, cars, streets, and project backyard brawls. He told me if I listened hard enough, I could hear her heart beating

73

in the apartment next door. I'd know she was okay. Her father hadn't gotten to her tonight. Maybe I could save her tomorrow. Her father always seemed to get to her mother, though. Ms. Linda was a pretty woman who went to church with my mother on Wednesday nights. She had eyes as bright as the diamonds in the big chandelier at the Macy's downtown, a wide happy smile she'd given to Muriel, and hands as soft as clouds.

Muriel's father, Mr. Johnson, wasn't pretty. He never played or smiled. His eyes were dull like the eyes of the dead dog Muriel and I found in the alley one day. And his hands were hard as bricks. I never touched them. Never wanted to. But something so, black and angry couldn't have hands like clouds. His hands broke things. Banged things. Could tear through project cinder block walls. I could hear those hands at night, boxing on Ms. Linda. Bruising her diamond eyes. Bloodying her lips so she tasted salt when she smiled.

No matter how hard I tried, I couldn't understand why he did this—not that there could be a reason to hit a woman, especially a woman as pretty as Ms. Linda, but when you're eight years old, you expect there's an explanation for everything God allows. I couldn't find one. Ms. Linda cooked the best dinner. She had a plate of food ready on the table before Mr. Johnson got home. Every day when he walked in the door, everybody snapped to attention.

Muriel always begged me to stay for dinner, so I could be there when he got home. She said he wouldn't show out quite as badly when somebody was in the apartment. And it couldn't be just anybody. At one time, the Johnsons had lots of friends, but he'd run them off. He'd drink from the square tin in his shirt pocket and shout about visiting imperialists coming to plunder what little he had left from all of his hard work. He said they were assassins of dignity.

He never rapped anything like that when I was there, though. My mother said it was something about respecting my father. Both of them were from the South. Both of them worked with their hands. Both of them fought with the world every day.

"What we having for dinner, Linda?" he asked one night after Muriel and I had been sent to wash our hands.

At the sink, I could hear Muriel's stomach growling. I was already full. My mother fed me an hour or so before I had to go next door to save Muriel and Ms. Linda. She'd told me to take the smallest piece of meat and holler like hell if Mr. Johnson started cutting the fool.

Muriel was three whole years older than me. When we were little, our mothers used to make us hold hands and would call us best friends. But now Muriel was taller than me. Her braids grew longer every summer and something that looked like two fat grapes or Ping-Pong balls were poking through her T-shirt. I had no idea what they were, but I couldn't stop looking at them. Couldn't stop looking at her. Thinking about her. She was my best friend. But she wouldn't hold my hand anymore.

"Chicken! Again?" Mr. Johnson was laughing when Muriel and I got back to the wobbly wooden table in the kitchen. "Steak is what a man needs when he gets in from them streets. Steak's what he needs. Steak and lobster." He looked at me. "You hear me, Lil DJ?" He laughed louder like he was imagining I was my father. "Downtown, them White boys who get in my cab call it 'surf and turf.' See, that means food from the sea. Food from the land. A White boy don't want food from no coop. He wants food from the open world. From the sea. From the land. His woman give him both every night. My woman give me this. My woman want me in a coop." He laughed again and I did as well. Laughed like I thought my father might have.

"I give you this 'cause I love you, Clarence," Ms. Linda said, her shaking hand waving over the bowl of skinny fried chicken parts like some magic trick could turn it to something they eat downtown.

"Do you love me? Do you really love me?" he asked, stabbing the biggest breast of the bird with a fork held face down in his hand. "No way you could. No way you could love something big, black and ugly from a coop."

I prayed at church for Muriel. One Sunday morning, my father, my mother and I were sitting in a pew right across from Muriel and her mother—Mr. Johnson never came to church. Pastor Johnny Spokegood was in the pulpit talking about laying your burdens down. Sweat was rolling off the sides of his face and falling on the deacons in the front row. Muriel had on a dress the color of plum skin and matching silky ribbons in her hair. Her mother's cheek was less swollen than the day before—"just enough to come on to church," I'd heard my mother say.

"Go to God on your knees in the morning, scream and shout a praise song at night. Prayer is man's song to God. Prayer changes things. And if two shall touch and agree, it will be done. Lay your burdens down on the altar. Lay your burdens down and watch God work." Pastor Spokegood seemed like he was speaking to Muriel and me. We needed Mr. Johnson to change. We needed him to know God like Pastor Spokegood and the deacons in the front row. My father needed him to come to church. Sing a song to God. Maybe Mr. Johnson wouldn't beat Ms. Linda so bad then. Maybe he'd let Muriel rest and not cry and be so sad throughout the night. We needed to touch and agree. We needed to lay our burdens down and watch God work.

I looked over at Muriel in the other pew. She was looking back at me. I put my hand out in the aisle to reach hers. I watched her fingers move a bit. I swear I saw her hand reach for mines too.

"Pay attention!" her mother said, plucking her on the forehead. "Pay attention to God."

Ms. Linda shot me a stare.

I turned away in time to see my father jump to his feet and fall to his knees.

My father always said that as long as I lived in his house, I had to have to work. After, he was recited his story about being out in the fire-hot fields in Tuscaloosa, Alabama, picking cotton and bleeding baby pigs by the time he was eight. My mother convinced him that taking out the trash was job enough for a boy born in the city. Things were different now. They'd come North looking for change, and while neither one of them had finished junior high school, my mother kept talking about me going to a place called "college."

"Ain't gonna be no need for him to know how to bleed no pig or pick no cotton in college, David," she'd say as sweet as if she was sending me to heaven. "There he's gonna need his mind. His mind big and strong." She handed me the garbage and stood in the doorway to watch me walk outside to the trash chute.

My father used to drive cabs downtown like Mr. Johnson, but one day he said he got tired of moving faster when he saw a White man raise his hand while standing on the side of the street. One day he said those streets started looking more like rows on a plantation and his hands rounding over that steering wheel seemed ready to pluck another soft white ball of American gold. He said that on that day he decided he couldn't keep driving men around so they could make big decisions. He was a man. He needed to make big decisions.

My father decided to learn everything he could about those cars that drove the white men around the city. He would learn to fix them. As the owner of David Jenkins' Elite Car Service. He bought broken cars at half price and fixed them up. He would decide who came and went in the city and how they got through it.

It was his "big plan," my mother always said when it seemed he was down and forgetting, he just needed a little reminding.

I knew better than to get into their conversation, but I'd nod along with my mother in case my father needed me to also believe. It seemed like something was always getting in the way of his big plan, his way to make his own decisions, and it wouldn't be until I was much older and out in the world on my own before I understood what it was. A man with little education can hardly have his way with big plans. Especially if he's Black.

In order for my father to become a certified auto mechanic, he had to pass a test. Of course he knew everything about those cars. Every man in our neighborhood did, including Mr. Johnson. But knowing what's on a test and passing a test are two different things.

Tests frustrated my father. Made him nervous. Made him forget everything he knew. Made him angry. He already failed the test two times. And my mother was talking about the third being the charm.

"You know your father missed this thing—he missed this idea," she said, squinting over her glasses at the first page of a practice test he'd taken before he'd left for work. I was sitting beside her at the kitchen table doing my reading for school. She'd started coaching him after he failed the test the first time. Helping him understand what the words on the test meant. She said he had to get the idea— the main idea of the question in order to answer it correctly.

She erased his answer and wrote a note in pencil in the margin. I listened to her exhale and watched the frown settle across her forehead before she moved to erase the next answer and then the next.

"Do you think he's ever gonna pass that test Mama?" I asked.

"Of course he will," she said, not looking up. "He has to. I've prayed about it."

"But… what if he doesn't?"

"He has to." She looked up at me. "Your face is troubled, darling." She cupped my chin with her hand, softened her eyes. "You don't need to worry about this old test. It's only a wall. And exactly like your daddy did to get us to where we are now; he's gonna knock it down. We have to maintain our faith. Me and you together. We touch and agree. And you know what?" She slid her glasses off her face and turned her chair all the way to mine. "Soon we gonna leave this place. Go someplace better. We're gonna get our own apartment. Our own place where there ain't no roaches or piss in the street and the elevator. No screaming women or crazy men."

"We leaving Harlem?" I asked.

"Darling, I don't know if we'll get that far, but we're leaving the projects. Going across town where your daddy can own something. And the state ain't trying to run him off. Won't that be nice? My own kitchen. A bedroom for you. You won't have to sleep in the living room no more." She pointed at my bed, which was really a cot, propped up against a wall five feet from the kitchen table.

My mind went from my father's troubles to Muriel's.

"Can Muriel come with us? She can stay in the room with me."

She laughed. "No, darling. She got her own family. Her own mama and papa."

"But what about Mr. Johnson? What if he hits her?"

"We're working on him," she said. "And don't you worry about that. He got some suffering in him. Stuff he can't climb over. But we're working on him. Praying every day. And everything's gonna be all right."

Like my mother said, the third time was the charm. My father passed his test and we were moving out of the projects and on to the next point in his big plan. His troubles were over and he fired up the grill in the back of the building to prove it.

The sun had gone down and my mother and Ms. Linda were sitting at one of the stone picnic tables eating potato salad and hot dogs as they laughed about everything.

Muriel was sitting beside her mother. The summer sun had darkened her skin a shade browner, making it more radiant than it had ever been. I decided we'd get married and I'd look at her pretty skin every day.

"DJ, pay attention to what you're doing now." My father poked me in the shoulder. He was loading ribs onto a plate I was holding with both hands. "I paid good money for this meat and I don't intend to see it nowhere wasted on God's earth."

I walked the tray of hot meat over to the table where the women were sitting and put it beside the pile of hot dogs. My mother was telling Ms. Linda about the new curtains she was buying for her "very own kitchen" in her "very own apartment."

I walked backwards to the grill, keeping my eyes on Muriel the whole time. I couldn't leave her here alone. Not with him. She had to come with us to the new place with the new curtains. We could get married. She could stay in my bedroom. We just needed to agree. I reached for her. I saw her hand move a little. I swear I saw her reach for me.

"DJ, pay attention to where you're going," my father snapped as I walked up on his heels as he stood at the grill. I turned quickly and excused myself quickly. My father was country. And, unlike my mother, he still believed in a religion where beating children who got out of line was ordered by God. And getting out of line was equivalent to getting in his space. "I don't know what's gotten into you today. You seem distracted. Got your eyes everyplace but where they need to be. That girl ain't hardly thinking about you."

"Oh, David, stop it. Don't tease the boy," my mother ordered him, laughing with Ms. Linda as I turned red. "It's a little crush. It's cute. He don't want to lose his best friend."

Muriel looked away. So did I.

My eyes found the doorway right past the grill. There was a big black figure forming a shadow. Mr. Johnson was only recognizable due to the size of his frame and the way he rocked back and forth as he stood idle. His bouts of suffering had gone away for a while, but when news of my father's test came, I heard the screaming on the other side of the wall again. He was growling like a wild dog.

"Clarence! That you in that doorway?" My father called to the shadow. "Come on over here and get you something to eat, country boy. It's my celebration. I got good meat. Fill you up."

"You got good meat?" The darkness moved and Mr. Johnson emerged with the friendly smile he always had for my father. In the corner of my eye, I saw Muriel and Ms. Linda straighten up. My mother put her arm around Ms. Linda.

"That's right! Got ribs for us men. Hot dogs and buns for the children and women," my father joked.

"Lord knows you're joking, David Jenkins. Hard as I worked on that test with you, I'm getting me some ribs. Me and Linda getting some ribs!" My mother laughed and snatched the smallest rib from the pile. She slid the tray over to Ms. Linda. "Go on, Linda. Get you one."

The woman, who mere seconds ago was laughing and alive like my mother, didn't move before looking at Mr. Johnson for an answer.

"Oh, y'all stop all that now," my mother scoffed. "Can't she have a rib, Clarence? Ain't you gonna let your beautiful wife have a rib? She prettier than me. Prettier than any woman out here. Can cook better, too." My mother jabbed at Ms. Linda's side playfully and she let out a little humble laugh. "Don't she deserve some good eating?"

"Okay," Mr. Johnson agreed with a grunt.

When the charcoal burned to a white dust, our bellies were filled and the chatty women along with Muriel went inside, I was sitting on top of the picnic table beside my father and Mr. Johnson. They were sipping beer and talking about the trouble they knew in the South and found in the North. It was getting late, so almost nobody was left outside. The projects got dangerous at night. And it could only be safe out there for strong men. And evil men. And boys who were lucky enough to have fathers who were one of the two.

"I knew you was gon' pass that lil test. Yo' missus works so hard. I hear her praying through the walls every night for you. She's talking and praying and talking to you and praying to God. That's a good woman. She loves you."

"She loves me as much as I love her. The key is in treating her right."

"Go 'head, go 'head with that, brother," Mr. Johnson broke in, slurring a little. "The woman's eyes were like the world. She don't love what's Black no matter how you treat her. You try being as big and Black as me and you see what lovin' you get from the world. They'd make a whole new test for me to fail. Need me to stay in my place. And she'd make sure to keep me there."

My father gazed up at the sky. He always said a man couldn't convince another man to change his mind. Not even a strong man. That was God's job. One man could only point the other man in the right direction.

"Linda always saying I ain't thinking right. And I need to let go of the past and what's hauntin' me," Mr. Johnson went on. "She say she love me so much. But that pretty one can't love a thing like me as much as she say. She can't. She trying to make me forget the lessons I done learned. But I got something for her. Something she can't take from me." Mr. Johnson pulled a little dusty sack from his back pocket.

"What you got in that old sack, Clarence?" My father asked.

"It's my dirt. I took it out the ground before I left North Carolina and keep it with me. Right in my pocket. I keep it to remind myself of who I am and where I'm from, so can't nobody make me forget. After I bathe, I put the sack back in my pocket, so I always know. So I don't forget. If I do, I start thinking the world is too kind and loves me. I lose my fight; they'll take my Black ass and string me up in a tree like they did my daddy. I ain't gonna forget. I ain't ever gonna forget. And if my mind tries to, I have my sack." He flipped the dirt sack up in the air in front of him like it was a gold coin and returned it to his pocket.

It was about time for my father to say something, but he didn't. He just kept looking up.

Mr. Johnson finished his beer and sucked his teeth until he got out whatever meat was left in his gap.

It was getting darker. Darker than any night I'd ever been allowed to see in person and I was about to ask to go inside. But then my father spoke.

"I think we need to pray," he said.

"Pray?" Mr. Johnson looked at him—not like he was crazy, but like how I looked at my father sometimes.

"We need to pray," my father affirmed. He didn't wait for us to answer. He got up from the table and went to his knees.

Mr. Johnson looked at me.

I stood up and crept down to the ground beside my father.

And then Mr. Johnson did, too.

"Do I have to bow my head?" I asked, wondering how many people were watching this strange sight from their windows—two Black men and a boy on their knees in the Harlem night.

"Of course," he said. "We have to show respect." He put a gentle hand over my head and lowered it. Mr. Johnson's head lowered as well and I was surprised. Figured it was the liquor from the tin and beer that had him following along. I'd never seen him pray. Never once seen him on his knees.

"Dear Lord," my father started as he always did, his voice echoing as it bounced off of the concrete around us in the courtyard. "We need you here right now. We need you to erase evil and suffering from the hearts of men right now. We are good men. We are strong men. We worship you. We give you praise. We need you here right now."

My father prayed Scripture from his head and from his heart. He asked for deliverance. He asked for guidance. He asked for it all in Jesus' name and hollered like the outside world was our church. I felt like every star in the sky was someone who needed to be out there with us. Muriel was the farthest North. The concrete was a chorus. Something was moving all around. A breeze. A gust of power. The feeling of my mother's hand on my chin. There was comfort everywhere.

Mr. Johnson got off his knees more drunk than he had been when he'd knelt down to pray. He could hardly stand, but seemed in a rush to get inside. He thanked my father flatly and padded to the door.

A stream of brown dirt trickled from his back pocket.

"Times will change," my father said.

"Are you sure?" I asked.

He touched my hand.

"Now, they have to."

That night, I slept closest to the wall in the living room—with my ear cradled to the coldest part of the cinder block where Muriel's bed touched mine on the other side. I couldn't go to sleep. In the morning, we were leaving, packing our things in a big truck and leaving Muriel and her cries behind. I had to figure out a way to have her come with me. I had an empty box beside my bed and if I heard her cry out, I'd punch through the wall and pull her to my side. Put her in the box and take her away from her daddy. I'd marry her if she would let me.

I prayed every word I'd heard my father send into the night. I listened to her father screaming. Listened to her mother screaming. Heard things I'd never heard before. Babies two floors down. Cars out in the street. Junk. And mess. Anger. And fear. I listened and prayed and soon it all went quiet. Then, there was just Muriel and me. On two sides of the wall. Just us. Her heart was beating faster. I put my hand on the wall in the space where she must have been lying and crying. And I swear I felt her reach for me.

"Jesus, please fix Mr. Johnson," I said.

"Oh, Jesus!" I heard my mother yell and the light came on in the living room where my bed was against the wall. "What's all that screaming? What done got into Clarence tonight?"

She was rushing around and pulling on her clothes and then I heard the screaming louder still.

My father came out of the room. "What are you doing?" He asked my mother.

"He's gonna kill her! You hear that? He's gonna kill her! I have to go over there!"

Now there was knocking and screaming coming from the other side of the wall.

"Muriel," I thought as I jumped out of bed and ran behind my mother.

My father went into the bedroom and came back out with his gun in his hand. We left our door open and went to Muriel's. My mother tried to knock, but there was no answer. More screaming and knocking. Screaming so loud. Cries.

My father kicked in the door so loud it sounded like the gun had gone off and we spilled into the apartment where I pretended to eat dinner every night to save Ms. Linda and Muriel.

"Don't hurt her!" My mother yelled, but I don't think she knew yet what we were seeing.

Mr. Johnson was on the floor and Ms. Linda was standing over him. He was shaking bad. Shaking real bad and speaking like they did in church. Speaking in tongues. Dirt was all over the floor. On his hands. In his eyes.

Muriel ran over and grabbed my hand.

"I heard you praying," she said. "I prayed, too."

"What's going on?" My mother cried.

"I found him like this," Ms. Linda said. "Found him calling on the Lord and shouting in the night."

My father fell to his knees and started praying.

"He has the Spirit," my mother mouthed and her voice was nothing above a whisper. "The Spirit is upon him."

Mr. Johnson's big body was shaking like a baby and his chest was convulsing up toward the ceiling like something was threatening to come right out of him. His voice was like thunder.

My father got ahold of his feet. My mother grabbed one of his arms. Ms. Linda took the other. But he kept shaking.

Muriel and I fell to the floor holding hands. Our knees hit the old dirt and it seemed we'd been shown places we'd never seen. Those places of trouble and struggle. Dark corners. Ugly things. Lies.

The screams were so loud they rattled my bones, but I held tight to Muriel's hand. I held her hand and prayed like my father did. Like my mother did. Like Pastor Spokegood said to. I prayed for what seemed like all night.

And then there was light. The sun came up. Mr. Johnson had gone to sleep.

Muriel didn't have to get in that empty box. And I didn't have to steal her away and marry her when we moved. Her father was still big and black, but anger left him after that night. He accepted Ms. Linda's soft, cloud hands all around him. He smiled at more people, more than just my father and me. There was no more dirt sack from North Carolina in his back pocket. The dirt, every speck of it scattered on the kitchen floor, and even those that left a trail outside burned like tiny hot coals and left pockmarks in their wake. Some people called it a miracle. My mother called it God.

My father's big plan moved us into our apartment and then into a condo and then a brownstone on Hamilton Terrace where my mother put new curtains in seven kitchen windows. "Seven windows," she was always saying. "I have seven windows in my kitchen." She kept praying and talking to my father. She was always there to help him and it seemed her love alone, her faith, kept him focused. David Jenkins' Elite Car Service was one of Uptown's top cab companies. Now, he was talking about moving on to Midtown. Then Downtown.

In my new neighborhood, I met a lot of girls who were as pretty as Muriel. As kind as Muriel. Girls who didn't have angry fathers who suffered. Girls whose fathers made decisions and owned brownstones like mine where their mothers could decorate windows with new curtains. I met them all. I dated some. But, still I listened for Muriel's heartbeat in everything. Everywhere I went, I listened. And it never left me. The tempo pulled me closer to God and there I heard His voice telling me to be still and keep praying over whatever noise was around me. She was my peace in a world that seemed to have as many big plans for me as I had for myself.

I did go and try to see her a few times. But as she grew, it seemed time was pulling her away from me. And no matter how I grew and thought that "Now I'm big enough for her," she'd be bigger still. Then, one Sunday afternoon, Ms. Linda invited me over for dinner. She said it would be a nice surprise for Muriel. I showed up with flowers in my hand. I showed up ready to ask Muriel to be my girlfriend. I was thirteen. I could take her to the movies. I could speak without squeaking. But when I got there, another boy was there. He was bigger than me. His name was Winston. He'd moved to

America from Jamaica and was darker than Mr. Johnson. He had something called "dreadlocks" in his hair and made Muriel laugh when he said her name, curling the "u" with his lips. She told him I was the little boy who used to live next door. I saw him put his hand on her knee under the table. I told Ms. Linda the flowers were for her.

On a cold afternoon in March when I was in my final year at college in Stony Brook and my mother had one of my father's drivers carry her all the way to the island to meet me for lunch, she said she'd heard from Ms. Linda from the old projects.

"She said I should send her thanks to you," my mother said, smiling. "She thinks you and your father saved her husband's life—saved her life, too."

I was about to ask about Muriel, but my mother didn't give me a chance.

"And Muriel's in college. Went down to Georgia to go to a school called Spelman. You heard of that college? Linda says it's a good school. Muriel got a full scholarship. She's graduating and coming back to New York." My mother was silent as she looked intently at my face and waited my response.

"Yes Mama, I have heard of that school," I answered, imagining what Muriel must look like now. If she still knew Winston. If she ever thought of me on the other side of the wall.

My mother slid a slip of paper onto the table and suddenly I realized why she'd come all the way to Stony Brook to have lunch with me.

"I want you to write to her, darling. Write to your Muriel."

"But mama, that was so long ago. I don't think she'll even remember —"

"You ain't been in love once." She cut me off. "Ain't been in love once. Ain't even bring no girl home. That's because you're waiting for Muriel."

"No. I—"

"Son, your heart is waiting for Muriel. I prayed about it. I know." She pushed the paper closer to my turkey sandwich. "Write to her, son. Listen to your mama." It was an order under the guise of a request.

We bowed our heads and prayed before we ate.

That night, I tried writing to a Muriel I didn't know. I hadn't seen. It was tougher than writing any paper. Tougher than Socrates and Milton. Statistics and physics. So many words were in my head, I got a headache and when I thought I'd said enough, I looked down at the page and there was nothing. I cursed the paper and my mother for giving me the address. What was I to say? I was a man now. This was the love from my boyhood. What was in my heart then was silly. Childish. I couldn't save Muriel anymore than she could save herself. I was just pretending to be her protector on the other side of the wall. And then I imagined that I was that boy again. I remembered what Muriel looked like. Her diamond eyes like her mother's. Her wide, happy smile. Those long braids. Then, I started writing:

Dear Muriel,
I am still here for you. My heart is still here for you if you reach for it. — DJ

And that was it. There was no "How are you?" or "What have you been up to?" There was no easy way to say what the boy in me knew I needed to ask to that woman. She was still my heart and I'd learned long ago that there could be no pretense where the heart was concerned.

I folded the letter and dropped it into the mailbox before something smart in me said not to.

Two weeks later, my roommate dropped a response on my bed. Muriel had drawn a flower on the envelope.

Dear DJ:
My heart is humbled by your words. Humbled that you haven't changed. Happy that you haven't changed and that you can still feel me reaching for you. I am coming home at the end of the month. Won't you come over for dinner? — Love Muriel

I looked at the calendar over my desk. It was a Tuesday. When my semester ended two days later, I got in my car and drove to Atlanta.

Muriel told the story of finding me in the lobby of her dorm to everyone at our wedding. It's her favorite story. She wasn't sure if it was me at first. She says I looked so much taller and had muscles in my arms and a beard. But the face, my face, was familiar. She dropped her book bag. She started to cry and fell into my arms. She asked if I would stay until it was time for her to come home. I told her I hadn't planned on leaving.

"When we were little, our mothers made us hold hands and called us best friends," Muriel said, standing beside me in her white dress. "And they were right. DJ, you were the best thing for me when I was at my worst. You saved me. You saved my family. And I know God put you in my life for me to love you. I know this is right. God made you for me. God made me for you."

I cried; I was helpless; I couldn't say a word.

My father, the best man I knew, was standing behind me. Mr. Johnson, the man who'd given Muriel away to me, was standing beside her. Our mothers were in the front row crying, holding hands, praying and agreeing.

I'LL ALWAYS BE LOOKING AT YOU

Amber Lovingmylifeeverday Jones: Mornin' FB fam! Spotted model Sazi Marimba at the airport here in Hawaii last night. She's so beautiful! Ugh. Made me want to throw my cheesy burrito away. :-/ She was with a bunch of photogs. Wonder what she's doing here on Big Island?

The sun had just come up over Punaluu Beach. Ebony was sitting so close to the water's edge the crashing waves played with his toes. The seat of the black slacks he'd been wearing since the night before was wet and sandy, but he didn't move. His head tilted to the coming waves, he inhaled the scent of the salted seawater in long drags. He could feel the cold water tickling his toes as it came in and receded again. His shirt, an ivory button-down, was open and the bottom seams sank into the wet sand all around him.

Others, those tourists wishing to see the beauty of the sunrise and witness Punaluu's watery opus before the day's crowds, ran away from the renegade rifts, but Ebony sat and let the scene play with him. The waves reminded him of time—first coming and erupting in white-capped, anxious, rolling ripples, then subsiding tranquilly in a soft song, retreating from the Big Island's richest black sand shoreline. He wondered where he fit into all of this. Was he coming or going? Or just somewhere in the middle?

In an hour, his crew would arrive at Punaluu. Five months spent searching for the perfect location to capture the shot his agent, Alex Bornstein, had said everything depended upon and this was it.

A week before the trip to Hawaii, Alex texted Ebony in the middle of the night, j: Did you update your Twitter? Let your followers know you're going to Hawaii. That you'll post pictures. They love that shit, man.

Ebony read it, but didn't respond. He slid the phone under his pillow and tried to go back into a dream of the Congo.

"Followers," he muttered. "I'm forty years old. What the hell do I care about followers?"

Two minutes later, Alex answered his own text: These young cats have pics up every day. Fifteen, twenty, fifty. They get the pics up and online, share them with their followers. What are YOU doing? What are WE doing? We have to keep up. The world is changing, man.

"Yeah. Yeah." Ebony went back to sleep.

The morning after the night text, Ebony sat in a coffee shop that was riddled with more laptops than coffee mugs, explaining to Alex why he wasn't on Facebook and didn't see the use in any photographer uploading dozens of pictures when it only took one to make the statement of many. It was one shot that got him to where he was. Wasn't it? Just one shot.

"The world is changing," Alex said, running his fingers through a rough patch in his jet-black hair plugs. He was forty-five. Divorced. And dating Inoko, a Japanese model, one of his clients, who was less than half his age. "People want information. They want to see it. See what you're working on. Who you're working with. They want it now. Like right now."

"You keep saying the same things, Alex. Like a tape recorder."

"That's the thing, man! The tape recorder is dead. Wake up." Alex pulled out his phone and updated his Twitter: Marrakesh Mint in Alphabet City w/top @TIME Mag #photographer @ebonyslaughter This brother IS it #FollowHim

LillyinPhilly1908: Ahh Alex is Jew? RT@agentalexb Marrakesh

Mint in Alphabet City w/top @TIME Mag #photographer
@ebonyslaughter This brother IS it #FollowHim

FitoLibroLookatmenow: Love his work RT @agentalexb
Marrakesh Mint in Alphabet City w/top @TIME Mag #photogra-
pher @ebonyslaughter This brother IS it #FollowHim

Ebony spoke of his desire for purity as Alex typed his status.
This online thing is a trend. It's going to stop. It has to. There's no
place for it in art. Artists aren't computers. We can't churn out work
to obey our followers. And what's a follower anyway? If I do this, if
I feed into this, I'll lose my soul.

"Your followers are dollar bills, Ebony! The ones that pay your
landlord. Your student loans. NYU, right?" Alex was checking his
Facebook and then shifted back to Twitter to see his responses.
He felt Ebony sigh and looked up. "Ebony, you're my best guy. The
best photographer out here, period. I know it. You know it. But who
cares if no one else knows? If no one sees? Help me help you."

Both Alex and Ebony laughed at this cliché agent pitch. Ebony's
long freeform locs and pierced ears were a sharp contrast from
Alex's sleek Armani suits and slicked back hair that almost made
him look Italian. The pair met ten years ago at Ebony's first major
exhibit in SoHo; they'd become close friends over the years and
trusted each other in ways and for reasons they couldn't explain.

For three years, Alex couldn't find Ebony any substantial work,
just small catalog and photoshoots for publications no one had ever
heard of, but then Time magazine organized a team of photographers to send to Congo. Alex signed Ebony up for what they thought
would be a photographer assistant position. Then he met Sazi. And
everything changed.

"Look, man," Alex started talking again as he typed on his phone.
"I'm your guy. You say you want to keep it pure. You do it. But you
have to give me something. And fast. These young cats are moving.
You have to keep up. You get that beautiful girl of yours on that
plane to Hawaii and get me some shots of the most magnificent place
you can think of."

"She's not my girl," Ebony said, but he knew Alex hadn't heard him. He was busy typing on his phone.

Agentalexb: My man @Fito is best PR in Chi It's going 2 be big! Keep ur ears 2 the street #Follow @ebonyslaughter @FitoLibroLookatmenow @agentalexb

FitoLibroLookatmenow: Yo! #Follow my boy @ebonyslaughter He's NY's hottest #photographer

By the next morning, 873 of Fito's Twitter followers started to follow Ebony.

A crab dragging a huge white shell on his back crawled from a pool of soft black sand beside Ebony. The crab looked tired, but it made it. His whole life was with him. The contrast in color was brilliant. Ebony reached for his camera only to realize he'd left it at the hotel. There'd been a late-night welcoming luau with a fat, pink pig roasting on a fire pit the night before and afterwards Ebony never made it back to the hotel with the crew. He slept in the car behind the boardwalk, promising himself he'd wake up early enough to watch the sunrise.

A wave rolled in and took the crab and shell back into the ocean with it when it rolled back.

"I can't believe the sand is really black," Ebony heard Sazi say before he felt her soft, cool hand on his neck. He'd left her in the car, asleep on the backseat. "Like it's black. Really black," Sazi added.

She crouched down behind Ebony and began to squeeze his neck, gently and subtly as if she was preparing to massage him, and just as he was about to relax and turn around, she let go. She sat down, flipped her thin, long legs around his waist, nestled her chin into his shoulder. She was fifteen years younger than Ebony and he was acutely aware that unlike him, she still managed to move her body around without a groan or grunt.

She was also wearing her clothes from the luau—a thin black cocktail dress and stacked silver bracelets. Her legs were long and thin like tree branches. Her face was beautiful for a permanent shot. She wore a wide Afro that she sometimes parted down the middle and linked in two thick plaits. She couldn't believe they'd been around the world and never came here.

"It's so lovely," she said, placing her hand over Ebony's heart.

"That it is," Ebony said, catching her hand on his body before she slid it away.

They sat and looked for a while before Sazi asked, "You nervous about later? About the shoot?"

"As nervous as I should be," Ebony answered.

"Oh, stop it. Don't go sweating Alex and his demands."

"You're saying the shoot isn't important?"

"No, I'm saying it's not everything. It can't change everything. It's just —"

"I can't keep up—that's what Alex keeps saying." Ebony turned his head a little so he could see Sazi's profile behind him.

"With what?"

"The world. Everyone," Ebony said. "It used to be that I'd take a picture and it…it would mean something. Just that picture. But now, it's not about the pictures. It's not about the art. People only want what you can show them right now."

Ebony could feel Sazi exhale against his back. He looked back out at the ocean. Two women were playing in the water, snapping pictures with their cell phones.

@JenniferFleschner: Punaluu is star-studded! @Karen & I just spotted @SaziMarimba cuddling with some guy on our morning walk. I'm going to try to get some pics.

"I remember when we first met," Sazi started. "You came to Congo to take pictures of White girls with monkeys. I was eighteen, but I'd never seen anything like that—people out in the jungle taking pictures with the monkeys. I laughed so hard. Who wants to take pictures with monkeys? It didn't make sense."

Ebony could hear Sazi's accent now. She'd been away from home for so long, seven years, it came and went, was mixed with a brush of Saxony and Upper Westside pomp.

"I heard you laughing first... and then I saw you," Ebony said. He remembered her black skin. The tattoo of her tribe across her forehead. Eyes clear, but knowing. She looked ancient and new. Nothing and no one anywhere was like her.

"Yes," Sazi agreed. "You said I'd be rich if I just let you take my picture."

"You didn't believe me." Ebony grinned at the ocean.

"All I knew was war and me in the middle. People like you came and went. You were Black, but not Black. You were with them. White girls and monkeys." She paused, kissed him on the neck and moved away. "And you took my picture and you paid me. You took me to dinner. Asked why I was in the middle of the war in the Congo teaching. I was educated. I could speak English. I could leave. I told you about my parents. How they took me in when I was a baby. Loved me. Paid for my education. I couldn't leave them. I couldn't leave the other children like me."

Sazi's legs must've been tired. She released Ebony from her hold and let her legs fall to his sides. She leaned back and rested with her elbows in the sand like a man with nowhere to go. Ebony wanted to lean back into her, but he knew not to. She'd just move away.

"The morning when you were leaving, you told me you'd always said "I'll Always Be Looking At You." I thought I understood your English until I got the pictures in the mail. In every picture of me, I saw you looking at me. I saw me through you. And then the magazine came in the mail, too. There were no White girls with monkeys. Just me on the cover. 'Really See Inside Africa,' it read. In your letter, you asked if I'd ever seen America. Only in magazines, I responded. And then you sent a plane ticket."

A wave came in. It rolled past Ebony and touched Sazi's elbows. He felt her shudder. It took everything in him not to turn around and scoop all of her into his arms. He wanted to protect her. For her to protect him. The laughing girl he'd met in the Congo had grown into a full and complicated woman. Not just something he wanted to look at. Something he loved. He'd known this for a long time.

@BigIslandrazzi: '@JenniferFleschner Where on the beach is @ SaziMarimba? I'm coming

"I was so scared to come to New York. There were so many stories. Men hurting women. You know? Mother said to be careful," Sazi remembered. "But when I got off the plane, you gave me a check and keys to a place to stay."

"You earned it," Ebony said, feeling his body recline a little. "It was your money."

Sazi came up again and pushed his back up straight. Before he could react, she wrapped her arms around his chest. His tight muscles pulsated as he breathed. She went on about New York—the people, the crowded streets, the buildings. The work and finally understanding that she was being paid to have her picture taken. Other photographers were cheating the models. Taking their money. Sleeping with them. Using them. So many horror stories.

Ebony half-listened. He'd heard Sazi tell this story before. By now, he'd learned every one of her stories. He'd learned her. How she didn't mind being intimate with him, touching him, but avoided his full intimacy. She'd say they were friends. Laugh him off. Get up and go. Run away. Then come back and wrap her arms around him. This should make him mad—Alex said, often. He'd given her everything. Right? Why couldn't she at least let him hold her at night?

"She's playing with you, letting some other brother hit it while you're busy making her rich, man."

Ebony couldn't see this, though. Over the years they'd worked together, there had been no other men. Most nights, Sazi was peacefully sleeping on his couch. He watched her. He wanted to touch her.

@CarlosissoBK: Post pics #BigIsland I want 2 C that sweet thing @SaziMarimba is w/ photog #Follow @EbonySlaughter @Bigislandrazzi @JenniferFleschner

@BigIslandrazzi: Hey @CarlosissoBK On my way 2 #Punaluu 2 check it out Now! Might have some #photos up by lunch time

Morning was leaving them. Soon the crew would be there. The models. The black steel and glass coming out of its case.

Ebony imagined Sazi in the black sand. Her smile. Her open eyes.

Her skin. She was moving in his mind. An easy distraction from his troubles. He felt his cell phone vibrate in his pocket and ignored it while turning to Sazi.

"So, what's making you think about home right now?" Ebony asked. Sazi always told the story of how they met when she was homesick. "You start talking like that and I think you want to leave me."

She replied, "It's not about me, Ebony. It's about you."

"Me?"

"I'm trying to remind you of who you are, so you don't forget. You're not like the rest of them. That's what makes you special. What makes your work special?"

"You're starting to sound like a Hallmark card."

Sazi playfully pushed Ebony away. He turned around to face her. Got up on his knees.

"Don't make fun of me," she said.

"I'm not. You're talking about the past. This is about the present. The future." He pointed out toward the ocean. "Who I was then doesn't matter. Does it? People care about right now."

So much had happened since the Congo. In New York, there were so many magazines. In London, so many runways. In Paris, in Italy, in Egypt, there were designers. They all had their lenses on Sazi, trying to capture a shot, one better than Ebony's. But none ever did. None could see her like he could.

He remembered the day he'd realized he'd fallen in love with her. They were leaving a party in New York. It was two weeks after her twenty-first birthday. The sun was coming up and she was complaining that it wasn't really a party at all. Just people talking.

"In my country, parties are places where family and friends resurrect relationships and rejuvenate the spirits of the ancestors," she'd said, her accent thick, her voice serious. "Parties are places for remembering and celebrating the words that we have shared with generations before and after us. Those people, those people in there, they just wanted to talk. They make unimportant commentaries and have empty conversations."

Ebony had wanted to kiss Sazi right then. He tried, but she recoiled.

She took his hand and whispered, "You could never really love a woman like me. You are confused by what you see." He had three glasses of wine and hardly heard this. He chalked it up to his age. How could someone so young and so beautiful love him? He'd hardly heard it, but never forgot what she'd said.

The women in the water stopped taking pictures of each other and turned to Ebony and Sazi. Ebony looked towards the beach and saw some new people running, but they looked like they were rushing toward something instead of working out. Behind them, on the boardwalk, a woman was typing away on her iPad.

"Let's walk," Ebony said, pulling Sazi out of the sand. Ever since Sazi had done her fifth *Vogue* cover and Vh1 had approached her about getting her own docu-series, Ebony had become accustomed to crowds closing in on them. People snapping pictures, wanting autographs. Sazi never seemed to mind. In fact, until someone got too close, she never seemed to notice.

Pictures were uploaded and over lunch, people in offices in New York and Atlanta were looking at Sazi strolling on the beach in Hawaii on bossip.com, the black gossip website. A post on Twitter mentioned Alex and included an article link. He was walking Inoko's poodle in Central Park when he saw it. Ebony was a shadow moving in the background.

@BigIslandrazzi: Check this out. #Photos @SaziMarimba @EbonySlaughter on the beach. Lover's weekend?

@CarlosissoBK: DAMN! Now, that's what I call a stunna! Post more #photos, @BigIslandrazzi

Sazi was walking ahead of Ebony and was smiling at things. More people walked toward her. They were pointing. Some taking pictures. Sazi smiled and stayed in her own world. Motioned with her finger for Ebony to come closer to her. She dashed ahead farther and jumped on a big black rock that was half in the sand and half in the ocean. The kind people stand on to take pictures.

"I will sit here on the rock and pose for you," Sazi said, grinning and dancing her shoulders back and forth. "Give Alex the perfect shot." Ebony remembered their first shoot. She was a woman, but shy as a girl. She kept walking away and disappearing into the bush. And sometimes, she'd be right in front of the camera, but Ebony couldn't tell the difference between her and the earth.

Something white and black had come into the shot. Ebony looked up to see that it was a zebra. Alone and standing still like it was already in a picture.

Sazi had spoken to the zebra in her native tongue. Ebony, naïve, afraid and excited, expected the zebra to hear her and do something beautiful. Bow and kiss her feet. It just ran away, disappearing into the bush like a deer being swallowed into a forest of green.

"That zebra didn't come to you when you called it," Ebony said over dinner that night.

"I didn't ask it to come to me," Sazi answered. "I told it to go away."

"I love you," Ebony said with a sudden eruption of emotion as he looked at Sazi standing on the black rock on the beach. His phone was vibrating again and he knew it was Alex but he couldn't look at it.

Sazi's shoulders fell. She turned to the water and looked up toward the sun while squinting her eyes. She put her hand over her eyebrows to block the glow.

"Hope no one's late for the shoot. The sun is—"

"I love you, Sazi," Ebony said, stopping her.

She exhaled, twisted around to the shore and came down from the rock in a huff like someone had been giving her a hard time.

"Let's go back. Drive back to the house and get ready."

"Sazi, I—"

"You're confused, Ebony! You don't know me," she said.

"We've been together for seven years. Hardly were we out of each other's sight for more than two days," Ebony said.

Sazi pushed past him.

He kept speaking. "What is it? I know you love me. Why won't you accept my love? Tell me! Tell me now!"

"This isn't even about me. You're nervous about the shoot. Trying to focus your attention somewhere else." She looked into his eyes. "Leave it alone."

"Why? You tell me one good reason why. I touch you; you run away. You won't let me get close to you unless you control everything. Where I put my hands. Is it my age?"

"You think that's what it is? Your age?" Sazi stopped and turned back to Ebony. She held her hands out to him. Tears rolled down her cheeks.

"Then what is it? You can tell me, Sazi." Ebony felt his heart breaking from the force of Sazi's tears. "I'm not going anywhere. Did something happen?" He finally thought that maybe there was something else.

In New York, Alex saw pictures of Sazi crying and looking at Ebony. He texted his client: "What's going on out there, man? I'm seeing pictures from everywhere. You OK?"

"You can't see me. Not all of me. That's why," Sazi said, wiping her tears as her bracelets clinging together on her wrist. One woman who'd tried to step forward from the growing crowd of gawkers to ask for Sazi's autograph decided not to.

"None of this means anything. Not you. Not the pictures. Not the people," Sazi cried, finally looking at the crowd, and from Ebony's angle, seeing them. "It's just an image. Just something to see." She paused and Ebony took her hand. "But there are things you can't see. Things you can't know."

"I will know if you tell me," Ebony said with a promise wrapped in his softest, most delicate voice. He thought to take her home. Get her away from the crowd and back into the car, on the plane and onto his couch where she could rest and he could watch and she could just be. Beautiful and still. But he knew that right then he had to let her unfold. He'd never seen this part of her before. "What happened to you, baby?"

"I lost a part of me. They took it from me."

"Who? What?"

"The people who loved me. They took it from me."

"Took what, baby?"

Sazi fell to the ground and her cries were so deep some people turned away or started crying themselves. Ebony bent over and took Sazi into his arms and tried to huddle her in his embrace.

"Let's get out of here," he whispered. "We can talk about this at the hotel. In private."

Sazi pushed him away angrily.

"No!" she shouted. "I'm tired of private. I'm tired of hiding from you... from everyone."

"Hiding what?"

"They cut me," Sazi managed. "They cut all of me away."

"Cut? What do you mean cut?" Ebony asked, wrapping his arms around her again, shielding her body beneath his chest. Then he saw her hand resting between her thighs atop her vagina. He looked and then stopped. Looked into Sazi's eyes. Through the tears he had stumbled upon a moment in her life as a girl he'd never even imagined. He'd heard about it and realized it happened in pockets and places in the world. Young girls cut up the middle like fish in some ancient ritual to preserve their youth but destroy their soul. Sazi? He wanted to scream her name. This image, the very idea, fell on Ebony like the heaviest wave in the ocean.

"Everything okay?" Sazi and Ebony heard from a voice in the crowd. Big Island, asking with genuine empathy, had shut his camera off and was standing in front of the crowd of photographers and onlookers, his hand reached out to Sazi.

"Everything's okay," Ebony said, still hawking over and partially protecting Sazi from view. "We just... we need a moment. You understand?"

The other photographers began to put their cameras away. Phones were turned off.

"Is she all right?" Jennifer asked, tossing her running jacket to Ebony. He placed it over Sazi's shoulders.

"I need to get her back to the hotel and—."

"No," Sazi erupted.

"What?" Ebony looked at her.

"No. I don't want to go back. I want you to." She flicked the jacket off. "You know what, do it now. Take my picture now."

"I can't. Don't be ridiculous, Sazi. You're upset. Not thinking straight," Ebony said. "Let's go back to the hotel."

Sazi rubbed her eyes and the mixture of black mascara and eyeliner that had already been streaming down her cheeks was now painted in wide circles.

"No!" she cried. "I don't want to go back to the hotel. I don't want to wait until later. Take it now. Take my picture now. This is who I am. This is what I am. Show me ... the real me!"

The photographers looked at Ebony as he stood halfway between standing and lifting Sazi from the wet sand.

"But I don't have my camera," he said. "See, I can't... I."

His phone was vibrating. It was Alex again. Had to be.

"You said you'd always be looking at me," Sazi said. "Look at me now. Look at all of me now! See inside of me."

"But I... I don't... We have to wait..."

The phone was vibrating.

Ebony put his hand over his pocket.

Sazi nodded for him.

"Do it," she said. "Show everyone."

Amber Jones @Lovingmylifeeverday: Mornin' FB fam! Looking at @SaziMarimba viral #photos MY heart is breaking 4 Her pics give me hope #MyWish we could be open w/ our scars

Time's photo of the year was taken on a cell phone on a black beach in Hawaii. The title reads: "See Inside of Sazi: One Model's Triumph After Genital Mutilation." The image was of Sazi in the sand. Her face marked as black as the earth. Tears mixed with salt water. There was no smile. No model gaze. The throngs of onlookers, their cameras held at their sides were in view. Sazi seemed to be reaching for the camera. Her heart in her hand.

When Ebony's name was mentioned among photographers on a short list for the Pulitzer Prize for Feature Photography, he and Sazi celebrated by announcing their engagement on their shared

Twitter page. They tweeted: From such sadness, comes such joy. We're expecting a baby.

Ebony didn't win the Pulitzer, but he managed to keep Alex's texts from arriving in the middle of the night. For a little while.

"You didn't lose your soul, man," Alex said to Ebony back at the laptop-filled coffeehouse. "You did the job, but kept yourself."

Ebony didn't saying anything. He smiled and took a sip of his tea.

"So, what's next? What are we doing next?" Alex asked.

"Nothing. I'm out of it," Ebony answered.

"No, don't say that again. You keep saying that and I think you want to leave me."

"Come on, Alex. It's time. If these young guys want to take this thing over, let them. My art is my art. And I'm not trying to compete for more followers or more attention."

"So, you're taking the job at Columbia?" Alex asked. Ebony interviewed with the university for a tenure-track position teaching contemporary photography.

"Yeah. I am. And I'm going to have my family. And love my wife. You know, our son is due any day now," Ebony said, seeing Sazi's full belly in his eyes. "And I'll still take pictures. I'm going with the flow. My own flow. What about you?"

WALL STREET WOMAN

Ten dozen, long-stemmed, and every color a rose could be. Vases were set on the floor, the window, the desk. The fragrance stepped out into the hallway like a man with somewhere special to go.

This grand gesture had wooed every woman who'd walked past Lana's office since the morning delivery. Lana, the one this spectacle was for, wouldn't see and smell it until the day was done and it was too late to simply say thank you. She couldn't have said thank you anyway. The sender hadn't given the deliveryman a name to include with the note. Just a message: Lana Lody—my Wall Street woman —Please see me.

"More coffee, Dr. Lody?" asked the middle-aged waiter with a white napkin placed perfectly over his arm. He wore a part down the middle of his unadorned scalp and gelled his thin strawberry blond hair behind his ears. His clients said it made him look younger. He moved closer and genuflected before the woman who was tapping away on a keyboard, seated at the back of the coffee bar. The shop was a few street corners away from her office filled with long stemmed roses of every color. He asked her again, "More coffee, Dr. Lody?"

"Yes, Bradley." Lana didn't look away from the figures glowing fluorescent shapes on her tortoise shell glasses from the laptop on the table in front of her. "And please..." She nodded to a mother sitting two tables over with a whining toddler bouncing on her lap.

"Certainly!" Bradley hustled away with his back still bent to ask the mother to excuse herself to another side of the bar. He counted his tips and explained that his clients came here to work early each day. There'd be meetings soon. It was a certain "kind" of crowd— he curled "kind" on his tongue like a foreign word. Didn't she understand? He would cover her expenditures.

The mother with the crying child gave Lana a stare of contempt. She couldn't believe someone like Lana could make something like this happen. In Bradley's suggestion, she heard exactly what she was supposed to hear—a demand. She would have to move. There could be no discussion. And angered though she may have been, she understood the situation.

This was a coffee bar with hard oak tables and dim desk lamps all around, private rooms, rows of executive Town Cars waiting in line outside at a busy New York City intersection, and $14 choice blends. She had to move and speak only through her eyes. Blue pupils set hard on Brown skin that didn't even notice her glare.

Lana clicked and tapped as the mother and child trudged off. She sat back in her chair and looked at the figures on the screen again, trying to see them, to see something in a new way that would explain everything. She missed her scheduled follow-up with her gynecologist and went instead to the coffee shop to work and she had already been at it for an hour. Plugging in numbers. Creating new definitions. Formulas. Hypotheses. Ideas. Ways to make it work. Yes, she could find a solution in numbers. It would just take some time. All she needed was more time. This was what she knew. How she understood she could make things work in the world. New numbers. New definitions. Ways of seeing. Time. Her first manager said this was what made her his best analyst. She had the mind and patience of a scientist. A love and passion for numbers.

After completing her Ph.D. at Harvard University, she'd taken the Graduate Management Admission Test as a joke. Wharton called her. Wall Street called next. Then there was the formula. The one that had made her first boss her first employee. Got her on the cover of the *Wall Street Journal*. Got her so many bouquets of lovely, smelly things she'd started having her assistant place them in cubicles around the office. Everyone wanted to say thanks, to offer up something, to wish her well. Former classmates, sorority sisters, that newspaper in Harlem, old colleagues, and old enemies—they all wrote notes and attached them to flowers as if she'd done something great.

Bradley slid the new coffee onto the table beside Lana's laptop as she was adjusting a long plait of thin brown dreadlocks over her shoulder. Her standard coffee order had a formula as complicated as the figures shone on her glasses: equal parts caffeinated and decaffeinated South African blend, steamed skim milk stirred in, no sugar—two teaspoons of dark agave nectar poured into the cup before the coffee, hazelnut creamer on the side—but with the first cup only, a sugar spoon on the saucer.

Bradley made it exactly as Lana explained each time, and every time she tasted it as if something was missing. "More agave perhaps, Dr. Lody?"

Bradley tried to read into Lana's pursed lips as they departed the cup's thin, green rim. Lana waved him off. She took another sip and clicked off the spinning ticker of instant messages her assistant had been sending from the office all morning: the doctor's office had called; her mother had called; flowers had been delivered; was she coming into the office today? Lana tried to pull the spreadsheet back up over the ticker, but something slowed the device so her eyes read the list of updates again. She clicked the spreadsheet again. Still nothing. A spinning pinwheel might have been more comforting. She hadn't saved her work yet and couldn't remember the last time she had.

There was a message from the doctor. Dr. Amiri, a gynecologist from Bangladesh who seemed surprised each year when Lana returned for her annual and revealed to him that, no, she wasn't pregnant. Last week his inquiry had gone past surprise, past warning. In a tight accent, he'd said, "You're forty, Lana. You must freeze your eggs if you ever want to be a mother."

He convinced Lana to let him do some tests. He took swabs, blood, and urine. He called back on Monday and made the follow-up appointment for this morning with Lana's assistant.

The spreadsheet popped back up just when Lana, in her mind sounding more like a teenager than a grown woman, had decided not to tell her mother anything about the doctor's appointment she missed.

An older Black man in a predictable Wall Street navy blue suit sat in the seat abandoned by the very noisy mother and child and was spending equal time sipping a cup of black coffee, reading the *Wall Street Journal,* and looking at Lana. She, of course, couldn't see this. She was looking at the bottom line now, considering how a five-percent deduction for investors might compel a better outcome for potential businesses. Maybe a signing percentage for the businesses? She flipped through some old sheets and then back again, sipped her coffee and pursed her lips. Something was missing. She couldn't see.

The ticker popped back up with a new instant message from the secretary at the office. She clicked it away without reading.

"You're that girl?" The old man finally said with his index finger pointed at Lana like she was a spot on a map. "I knew it! Yeah. Knew it when I sat down. From the *Journal* article. Right?" He almost smiled.

Bradley rushed in from a corner where he'd been watching and asked the old man if he needed anything. Was he ready for his bill?

The old man declined, excusing Bradley hard with his grey eyes that had once been brown when he was young and had less Scotch in his liver.

Still bent over, Bradley backed away into his corner.

"So how did you do it? Get all those companies to invest in those Black businesses?"

The old man went on as if he'd actually been chatting with Lana, but she'd hardly glanced at him to acknowledge the accuracy of his initial statement. "I mean, Osiris was obvious. You just had to put him out there. Package... Set numbers... A chain of upscale black male grooming lounges and haberdasheries... The consumer base was already there... Just needed a light on supplies... But the others? How'd you do it? Plug them all in?" The old man's eyes glittered and each new goal was marked with a kind of excitement one might expect from someone encountering the quarterback of last season's champion football team. Lana inferred he was likely someone in the business. A banker. Maybe an analyst like her. A business owner.

"You mind if I join you?" The old man picked up his mug and was about to slide over to the chair across from Lana when Bradley appeared between the old man and his destination with his bill. Not so gently, the man requested another cup of coffee. This time, he wanted a little sugar.

He was moving to shift seats again. Thought he remembered something in the article about Lana reapplying one of Carnegie's theories. Lana had to look up. "Sir, I'm so sorry. I'm kind of on a deadline." She raised her shoulders to indicate a predicament.

"Oh," the man said in a way that revealed that he was definitely an analyst. Definitely retired. And for some time now and had just come in and out of the rectangular maze of cold streets and corners to find what he'd once come there to locate. He set the mug down, nodded at Lana knowingly and went back to his copy of the *Journal*. There was a special report on laptop capers roaming throughout the city. Vagabonds waited for unsuspecting owners to abandon their technological devices in some seemingly safe place —a café, a library—snatch it and run.

Bradley came with a cup of new coffee and sugar. A new bill. He turned to Lana and asked if she needed anything. She'd been one of his regulars for five years now. He bragged about knowing her, serving her, to his friends. He felt less lonely when she was at one of his tables.

When he was gone again, the old man looked back at Lana, but in a different way this time. She pretended not to see and kept clicking and tapping. She sipped her coffee while her mind drifted a bit.

Osiris had been her classmate freshman year at Harvard. She couldn't forget his lips. Not how they looked, but how they demanded that she look at them in a way and for a long time, too. He was in the Black scholars program with her—the liberal citadel's way of giving back to the nation's brightest Blacks, and presumably needy. He was smart and poor and from Washington, D.C. She was smart and poor and from Brooklyn, New York. Both were the hope of an entire community of thirsty dreamers back home. Most mornings this pushed Lana to try harder, but soon she could hardly push past thoughts of what Osiris's lips must taste like. She missed the boy crazy era of puberty that left most of her school-aged friends pregnant and stuck in Bedford-Stuyvesant. Instead, she spent most of her days gaming with her brother, Lance, and thinking about speed over time, velocity, quantum theory, and other worlds. But now, seventeen and away from everything she'd already figured out, she was busy studying those lips and now those eyes. That voice. And now understood for sure how those bellies back in Bed-Stuy became so full.

A late-night study session led to Lana learning that, like her, Osiris was a gamer. He had beaten "Galactica's New World Order War" seven times while hiding from the war in the streets outside his parents' row house on Irving Street Lana admitted that she and her brother hadn't ever beaten the game. Something about the Goliath in the end. They'd tried for years. Osiris laughed and explained that it was about the tools he carefully placed in his character's backpack at each level. Not the big ones—hand grenades, machine guns and bombs (all the ones Lana and Lance had preferred in Bed-Stuy). He took the small ones. Bows. Arrows. Rocks. Then, when he got to the Blizzard Galactica Goliath in the end, he could take the Goliath down slowly to his knees. In that conversation, Lana decided that Osiris was the smartest person she knew. He wasn't a scientist like her, though. He wanted to major in business, open a barbershop like his father's. She'd thought it was a waste for such a mind. But he'd said it wasn't like any barbershop. It was something new. Something different. Lana kissed him when he said that. She licked his lips and vowed never to forget what it was like. But then, it seemed like almost immediately afterwards, Osiris announced that he was leaving Harvard for Howard University.

"Why?"

"This place has nothing to offer a Black man. I need to be smaller so I can get bigger."

Lana beat "Galactica's New World Order War" for the first time that night. She ran across campus to Osiris' room to tell him about her victory that had eluded her until that day. The door was unlocked. The bed was naked. She stood there scanning the room with her eyes, her arms at her sides and swore she'd never love a man like that again. And when she spoke it she realized she was in love.

Five years later, Lana learned through an e-mail that Osiris was opening his first grooming salon a few blocks from Howard. He wanted her to come. She couldn't.

The ticker reappeared over the spreadsheet interrupting her thoughts: you have to come smell the roses. They're amazing. Lana stabbed the mouse over the exit for the instant message program. She exhaled and clicked back to the spreadsheet.

"Small to big," she remembered Osiris telling her all those years ago in his dorm room. She looked at the bottom line. Three percent? More banks? It was all Osiris's idea. The big to small. Over the big to big. Simple numbers. Adding up. Just one figure needed to make the final number make sense. Pieces of armor. A war against the Goliath won by gathering the simplest tools that seemed to fail without each other.

"Darling," the old man called. "Darling?"

Lana looked right at him in time to see the last second of a stare at her bare left ring finger.

"Yes?"

"You married?"

"What?"

"Young girl... I mean, woman, are you married?"

"I... umm." Lana half laughed at this, but the show was more delightful than the thought in her mind. "Why?"

"Must take you a lot of time to figure out—"

"Look, Sir, I have to work."

He went on like he hadn't heard her. "I know you young people don't care about marriage and kids anymore, but what you seem to forget is that, none of those numbers you got there on that computer gonna make sense always. You need someone—people. You know?"

"Yes." Lana pretended to be calm. "I hear you, but nothing you're saying is going to help me right now. I have a meeting at five and my boss is going to want this done. So..." She smiled at the old man pleasantly like one of his grandchildren might. There was no meeting. She hadn't even decided if she was going back into the office. Maybe she couldn't. She needed more time.

"Yes, I understand," he said. "And, let me be clear, I'm not trying to discredit anything you've done. Those businesses would've shut down had you not—"

"It's fine. Really."

"I was just sitting here. An old scarecrow. You know? Looking at you and admiring your vision. Wondering what young man has the good fortune of sharing that vision."

Lana looked back at the screen.

It was all Osiris's formula. She wished they'd never written the *Journal* piece. All she did was click and tap. Plug it in.

She exhaled more deeply this time, slid the laptop back, then slid the coffee mug back, and looked at her perceived imposition.

"What about Osiris? Where is he? I'm sure he must be happy about you. You made him a millionaire. How'd you do it?"

Lana wasn't sure if this was the old man talking or her just hearing her own thoughts.

She looked up and the old man was gone.

The ticker reappeared: come see Dr. Lody.

Lana slammed the face of the laptop down and jumped up as the suits with eyes gathered around her.

"Everything okay Dr. Lody?" Bradley was there. Genuflecting.

"Fine." Lana's exhale was visible now. "I need a little air. I'm stepping outside. Look… watch my laptop for a second."

The air wasn't kind. It was chilly and not late enough in the autumn New York afternoon for last night's cold to have left the breeze.

Lana paced past a huddle of smokers and stood on the corner before the line of Town Cars. She hugged herself to avoid a gusty wind. A thick sweater she'd had since Wharton was left on the back of her chair inside the bar.

"Be cool, Lana. What's wrong with you? Focus." She looked around. The mother was crossing the street with one of those architectural strollers pushed out in front of her. She was a wife, Lana surmised, and had probably come into the city on the train to surprise her husband.

Dr. Amiri was wrong. There was nothing wrong with her. She simply needed more time. Why freeze her eggs? Forty didn't feel any different than thirty-five. And thirty-five hadn't felt any different than thirty.

He was trying to scare her. Plenty of women had children into their forties. There was that one woman on the news.

The old Black man in the predictable Wall Street suit helped the mother with the stroller onto the curb on the other side of the street. He smiled at his work and cooed at the baby.

I'm not even married. Why were so many people asking her why she hadn't had a child when she wasn't even married? Bisa asked if they could have children together, which caught her by surprise. Lana was sure she wasn't a lesbian and thought of the signals she must have mistakenly sent but when she welcomed the new experience. She certainly had not considered or wanted to have children with her hairstylist-turned-lover. Bisa was comfort, familiar and never left her in the middle of the night.

"Puff?" One of the other regulars asked Lana, holding out a lit cigarette.

Lana took it, inhaled, coughed, and handed it back.

When her mother asked about a man, asked about marriage, Lana got angry and found a reason to hang up the phone. Wasn't she enough? Her career? All of her work? She'd made it. Beat Goliath. Lance was back in Brooklyn driving buses. Lana had figured it out. Wasn't that enough?

The familiar face holding the cigarette tried to pass it back to Lana as he exhaled a thick cloud into the air between them. The smoke was comforting against the leftover chill, but the scent was abrupt and made her wonder for one second why, after smelling the smoke outside, anyone would want it inside of them. She held her hand up and stepped back.

She'd left Bisa in the middle of the night. Told her she needed to figure some things out.

Up on her elbows in the bed, Bisa seemed to refuse to connect Lana's gathering of things in the dark to something final.

"You're not even a lesbian," Bisa almost whispered. "I know."

The man with the cigarette was pointing at the glowing and vibrating cellphone on Lana's hip.

Lana smiled as if she had no choice because he was looking, she took the phone and pressed it against her ear.

"Been calling you all morning, Lana. How'd things go at the doctor? What'd he say?"

"Mommy, I told you I'd call you later. I'm at work." Lana backed away from the smokers.

"Just tell me what he said. Everything okay?"

"I'm at work. You never listen to me. I just told you that I'm busy." Mrs. Lody was saying something about the nerve of her only daughter to ignore her and speak to her in such a way, her voice faded, becoming background noise, and Lana's focus had shifted. She looked across the street and saw the old man and mother were still chatting. The old man pointing at the newspaper in his hand. The mother looking at Lana and shaking her head. Soon they both looked at Lana and became an assembly of frowns.

Lana hung up on her mother without saying goodbye.

She thought to run across the street and avenge her honor against the family of hecklers—now the baby was looking too. But to avenge what? She didn't even know what they were talking about. But inside? Inside, she thought of so many bad things she didn't want to hear. They had no right to say those things.

There had been men: business associates, fraternity brothers. She'd dated some for months and took some home to meet her mother, Lance and his wife and children—the twins... a boy and a girl (Lance's wife liked to point out that the boy was born first).

Some of these men even stayed the night, proposed something for the morning. Maybe breakfast or a walk through Central Park.

But Lana had things to do. She'd been too busy being too busy. And to stop? For what?

One of the partners at the firm had asked to have a child with her. He was forty-five and single, childless. She couldn't possibly want to be the same. "Now is a good time," he'd said. And with her brains? The woman who came up with the formula that was saving Black business from the behemoth depression? She was a genius. He'd consider it an honor.

Lana said no. That was too big.

The man with the cigarette pointed at Lana's hip again.

She answered ready to bark. She didn't even know the man at the firm. Not like that. And what gave that old man and mother a right to judge her decision? The paranoia was thick.

"I told you, I can't talk right now!" Lana spat into the phone.

"Dr. Lody?" There was a curious pause. "It's Dr. Amiri."

Pause.

"Dr. Lody, you missed your follow-up today. I need to see you."

The traffic light on the corner had changed and a band of taxis and somber black town cars began to move.

Cars began strolling by like a funeral procession.

"I'm working."

"I called your office. They said you hadn't been in this morning." Dr. Amiri's sigh was so grave, it nearly pulled Lana into traffic. "I really need to see you. Can you come in later?"

"For what?"

"Because I need to see you."

There was some commotion coming from inside the coffee bar. A shriek. What sounded like Bradley yelling, "Stop!"

Lana turned to the door in time to see it fling open and a man cradling a silver laptop to his chest padding out. He charged forward and nearly knocked Lana down.

She dropped her phone and went to get it as the man took off amid the confusion that at that moment seemed so fast, but later Lana would recall every detail—the smokers turning and pointing, the old man stepping into the street and yelling stop, Bradley coming out of the door behind the laptop cradler face red and ready to run.

"Get him! Get that man!" Bradley said to the crowd. He turned to Lana. "He has your laptop!"

"Mine?"

Lana started running with the phone in her hand down the street behind the man and the laptop. Fast. She couldn't see him sometimes, but then she could—turning the corner, crossing the street, down and out the alleyway.

"Stop him! Stop him! My laptop!" she hollered, feeling her heart thumping in her chest. She was out of breath, and he was still running, stopping sometimes to look back at Lana to see if she was still giving chase.

They stopped to rest. Eyeing each other from opposite sides of the street in an agreed stay.

"Who took your laptop, dear?" An old woman with a cane asked, standing beside Lana.

Lana couldn't speak. She pointed up the street to the man. He started running again and Lana was about to take off when the old woman handed her the cane.

"Beat him with this, dear!" she said. "He'll never steal again!"

So, Lana was running again, with her cell phone in one hand and a cane in the other. Heart flipping and her lungs pushing out the stale cigarette puff, cups and cups of coffee boiling in her belly.

The silver laptop almost ran into a pretzel stand, but the thief in his black hat and black shirt bobbed and weaved and escaped having only knocked one pretzel to the ground.

"Fuckin' asshole!" The man selling the pretzels at the stand yelled in his tough New York accent as he bent down to pick up the dirty baked bread when Lana ran up. "You fuckin' know him?" He asked Lana.

"No!" Lana managed. "Took my laptop… trying to get it!"

"Well, here!" Pretzel man handed Lana the dropped pretzel. "When you fuckin' catch his ass, you stuff this dirty pretzel right in his fuckin' mouth and tell him not to fuck with other people's shit!"

Lana could only nod.

She started running again. Up and over. Around the corner. Cell phone and a pretzel in one hand. The cane in the other. She couldn't see the laptop thief, but could tell where he'd gone by shrieks and stares of those around her. "That way!" some yelled. "This way!"

Lana ran harder. For what now, she didn't know. The man had taken something from her. Something silver. Something that glowed in her eyes.

And then she was at the great sea, the biggest intersection in the financial district where cars and bikes and cops and folks with faces from everywhere hustled around the Federal Reserve. She stopped and looked and looked. The faces and sounds told her nothing. Her head seemed to spin around in circles with her heart.

The phone was ringing again. Lana stuffed the pretzel into her pocket, looked at Dr. Amiri's number on the phone.

"Hello?"

"When can you come in?"

"I don't want to have a baby." She was out of breath but speaking clearly. "It's just too much. Too big." The city kept spinning around her.

"That's the thing, Dr. Lody. I don't know if you can." Dr. Amiri was padding as carefully as the man with the silver box at his chest. His voice sunk. "We should talk. I need you to come in. Can you do that? Later today?"

Lana looked around. "I'm in the office."

"No, you're not."

Lana abruptly clicked the phone off as tears fell from her eyes.

She couldn't be out of time. She grabbed the pretzel from her pocket and waved the cane in the air as she ran full speed ahead into traffic. The sea split right down the middle. Cars and people. Bikes and cops. They all moved, making a tunnel above ground leading right to the man with the laptop.

Lana's tears rolled into the wind. Everywhere was a battlefield. The wind toughened her skin like armor. The assailant would not escape.

Down the street he ran past a hotel with a guard standing out front in his thick red coat.

Lana almost ran into the guard but waved her cane just enough so he'd move out the way. But then there was someone else. A familiar form that seemed to come from nowhere and plant itself right in her path.

They both tumbled to the pavement. The pretzel flew into the street. The cane banged up against the hotel's sliding glass doors. The cell phone flew in the air and hit the payment with a cracking sound. "Oh no! I knocked you down!"

Lana was looking at the sky from the ground where she'd fallen face up and then she turned her head and she was looking at Osiris.

"Lana? You found me?"

"Osiris?"

"Why were you running?" He pulled Lana to her feet like she was a feather. His lips were the same. His eyes. "Did you get the flowers?"

Lana tried to look past Osiris to find what she was looking for, but she couldn't. She'd forgotten everything.

"Osiris?" Her heart was still pounding from the chase.

"Miss! Miss!" The man in the red coat came hustling back down the street toward the hotel. He'd chased the thief when he realized what was going on. "They caught him! The police! They caught the man with your laptop." He grabbed Lana's hand and pulled.

Lana was still looking at Osiris.

"It's just up the street a bit," the man said.

Lana looked at the man and then back at Osiris.

"I need you to come with me," she said.

"Where?" Osiris asked.

"I need you with me now. Can you come with me?" she asked.

"Yes. The answer has always been yes."

MELT

It was Saturday night in Atlanta and that music had been playing for hours. Slow, then fast. And once the drums went hollering and the bass moaned and dragged, it was somewhere in the hazy middle of the two. The result was a booming opera of hypnotizing sound that charmed hundreds of half-clothed entertainers to its stage, their sweat gathering on the wood beneath their feet.

The man was the leader. His arms might just be on the woman's shoulders gently pushing. And as soon as she was down, almost to his chest, he'd grind and set a speed. She'd ease in and quiver. His legs would spread out with the rhythm of the drums and maybe he'd turn her around. Arms crossed over her back, he'd bend her at the middle and she'd spin with the bass. Red fingernails reached toward the ceiling. Arms, black and brown and yellow, flailed in mock rapture. Shoulders in white tank tops and thin pink straps turned and tossed tick by tick. Hips in blue jeans and black miniskirts gyrated in rough circles at the floorboards. Everyone had their own way of moving to this music. Some slow and some fast. Some rude and nasty and some just opening up and playing shy. But all moving.

From above the wide dance floor, it was as if someone was painting one of those pictures where color and movement mix into a cloud of impression. Still, but changing. Some kind of human tapestry. And this was all because of the sound. A mix of everything. Hip-hop and Jazz. Salsa and Blues. Gospel and Soul. All chopped and minced

and gathered onto a soundtrack that spoke a melody never heard before. It was what would make Willie Colon would blush. What Féla could envy. And any MC should dream of rocking. And the DJ watched what DJ made. This sound—the music that had been playing for a while now and had the people in the fictitious painting swirling into a hip-grabbing hustle—was his musical experience on a soundtrack. He'd started all this five years ago when he was starving and trying to pay his bills so he didn't have to drop out of college and go back home to Memphis where his father said no preacher's son had any business being a DJ.

"And what is that music, Dax Jackson?" His father had asked, chucking holy water onto his first set of turntables. "I won't pay for you to go to college to be a heathen, playing heathen music. You're on your own." And that he was. Dax couldn't leave what he'd found on those turntables, and so the preacher's son became DJ and how he got by became a listening experience that knew no peer and called a crowd of heathens from everywhere. Liberty City. Wood Street. Fourth Ward. The Bottoms. West End. They came here to live here and move every weekend with him. They gripped hips and then turned again. They moaned with the bass and hollered with the drums. They looked at DJ and begged for more.

"Make me melt," they cried into the night.

And soon "Melt" was all there was. What he'd done to get by moved from his basement to the street, and from the street to the club. Now it was everywhere. "Melt" had become a movement.

Like many Saturdays before, there was a reporter there—a wiry White boy with rat-tailed red dreadlocks, tortoise shell glasses and a huge backpack holding a voice recorder and camera. He'd said he was a "believer" when he e-mailed DJ to request the interview. He had loved this sound since he was a misfit in Nebraska sitting at in his baby blue bedroom and dreaming of one day being here. A West Coast college escape and internship with the *Los Angeles Times* did the trick. He had a story to write.

"This is a trip! I listened to you when I was in high school, man! Have all of your old stuff!" He shouted all of this at DJ and then shrugged his shoulders, sure the man hadn't heard a word over the music.

DJ switched the track. Some Latin, almost African Melt that made the seemingly tired crowd pulse up and slap their hands at the floor. "Great, man," DJ said, but Elliot could only read his lips. His voice was flat and unaffected. He'd heard this so many times before from reporters who looked exactly like the one standing beside him in the booth.

He pulled his index finger, slow and in a circle, along the outer lining of a record spinning on the turntable. Another song began to play. He sat his headset on the only empty space in the booth and turned to the reporter, holding his hand out. "Dax Jackson," he said as another DJ came up behind him and picked up the headset. It was well past 2 a.m. and his set was up.

"Elliot Davis. *Los Angeles Times.* Hey, it's an honor."

DJ led Elliot down a thin, winding steel staircase that separated his booth from the dance floor. It was called the Movement Lounge outside on the door, but most people called it the Movement Room, because there was no open seat to lounge in at any corner in the square shaped place. And if dancers or onlookers wanted a break for their feet there was the concrete curb outside and the roof up above. No lounge in sight.

"So this is it," Elliot said, following behind DJ to the bar, his eyes wide and clear. "Where it all happens."

DJ smiled at the bartender, a blond haired, dark-skinned Latina whose English consisted only of drink orders. She reached past a crowd of pretty girls with short skirts and handed him two beers. They rolled their eyes at first, but then turning and seeing who was at the other side of the order, they blushed in their Brown skin and waved in a way that teenage girls with fake IDs do.

"Hey, DJ," they purred in a chorus.

He nodded.

"This thing is viral," Elliot said after thanking him for the beer. "It's everywhere. There's Melt in L.A. Melt in New York. Melt in South Africa… in yoga studios, man. Melt kissing. Melt sex. Melt weed!" Elliot laughed.

In those five years since DJ's sound first left his speaker, the soundtrack had long left this small place and primal start. And people would say, "Have you seen this? Have you heard that—how it is there—how it is way over there?" But to DJ it was all here. This was all there was. Yes, it was some big news to hear about the Melt club in South Africa, to get their invitations to come and play there, but there was always something different. Something not what he intended. What they were doing, what these people were putting off as Melt was just a copy. Just a reenactment of something they'd read or saw. They listened to the music. They learned the dances. But something wasn't real about it all.

"People can't get enough. They're listening. And that's why I had to come here. You know? To bring the essence of it all to paper. So people don't forget. So they know Dax Jackson and everything he's done for Melt. To tell the story the right way."

DJ found two barstools and the two men sat with their bodies facing the crowd. He kept nodding at Elliot's words. His plans. So many reporters with wide and clear eyes had come here to him before. They all wanted the story. They all had said they were "believers" in their e-mails. "Listeners." But in the end, all they really left with were some closed words about a new "craze." But that wasn't melt. That couldn't be it. And for a while, DJ just stopped letting them come altogether. The photographers. The reporters. What was the point? What could he tell them that they didn't already know? They maybe knew more than him. The history, the information, and the answers to the questions they all asked were on the computer. He couldn't tell them anything new. He wondered how Elliot had gotten here. Why he'd accepted his e-mail after deleting so many others.

"The right way?" DJ repeated Elliot's words. "What's the right way?"

"To be here! With the sound. With this…" Elliot pointed out to the dance floor. "To see what the music does to people. How it makes them move. How it captures them."

The men sat in silence and DJ watched his crowd. How they moved together. How they fed on the music and on each other.

Two women, each in little panties they called "Melt shorts," circled down to the floor and hunched until there was a crowd of men on top of them. The music went dim to DJ. His heart pulsated irregularly and he felt his center pulling him to the floor.

Suraya wore an Egyptian headdress and golden bikini top with roughly cut jean shorts to the club each Saturday night. She fell into the mass hunching the floor. She wrestled the men to their feet and ground her middle into them, one and then two, before dismissing them away. Suraya was the crowd teaser. Did nothing the way it supposed to be done. She made Melt her own universe where she was queen and the entire dance floor was her kingdom.

DJ watched and thought of what could take over these people in such a way. What delivered them to the dance floor and stole their inhibitions. Once the bodies touched, there was an extension, a connection that was so beautiful it had to be beyond purely sexual.

"It's my freedom," DJ heard Suraya saying as he looked into her eyes. She whispered this into his ear one night in the bathroom. Her legs cocked up over his hips. She promised she'd only ever love his music. She licked his earlobe and danced on him some more. "Make me free," she said.

"So do you want to wait to do the interview after the club closes? I need to ask you some questions—some specific things about the basement where you made the first recording and—"

"How does it capture you?" DJ asked before waving off some women who tried to invite him home after the late night.

"What? Melt?" Elliot looked at DJ. "I listen. It's in my head."

"No, this is about movement. You can't just listen. The music is about movement."

"Well, I'm not exactly a dancer. I love the music. But dance … No. No one wants to see that."

DJ's eyes trailed Suraya as she left the dance floor and moved toward a man near the other end of the bar. A quick glance over her shoulder at DJ to make sure he saw her followed by a smile acknowledging his eyes. DJ laughed and turned his attention back to Elliot.

"I'm a White boy from Nebraska," Elliot went on. "I can't go out there. I'm just—I'm here to help."

"You want to help?"

"I realize you don't give interviews anymore, DJ. I'm not even supposed to be here. And I know why." He leaned toward DJ and whispered to him. "You think they're—we're—taking what you made and turning it into some Walmart rollback sale. Get what you want out of it and keep it moving onto the next thing. But that's not it. The movement is real. And you can control it. You just have to have a message. And I want to help you share it."

"Well, my message is out there," DJ said, turning back to the dance floor. He got up from his stool and handed Elliot his empty beer bottle as he walked away. "It's not just the music. It's not just the dance. It's out there."

DJ didn't know he was looking for Suraya until he found her alone and smoking on the roof. Her legs were dangling over the front of the building.

"You gonna let that fool spin for the rest of the night?" She said without turning around. "Ain't nobody come here to hear his ass. He just wants to be you."

DJ didn't say anything. He crouched down and sat beside her. "I guess that's why you're out here."

"You knew I'd be up here. I came to hear you. Not into copies. I need the real thing inside of me. And who's the White boy? A reporter?"

"He's a believer."

"A fucking reporter. I hate that shit." Suraya offered DJ a puff of her joint and when he refused she flicked it off the roof.

"Don't be so hard, Ray," DJ said as Suraya finally turned to look him in the eye.

Suraya wasn't much younger than DJ. She dropped out of one of the colleges in the West End three years earlier and found an apartment around the corner from the Movement Room. She was Brown and had the face that reminded him of a cat. DJ always thought of how appropriate it was that she chose to wear Egyptian headdress, with her perfect tiny nose and secretive eyes. He had no idea what Nefertiti might look like, but looking at Suraya, he thought she had to look something like that.

"Hard?" She squinted. "Aren't you the one who stopped doing interviews? Who told the White boys with their cameras and recorders to leave us alone? That was you, right? Because maybe I'm confused."

Suraya's voice was biting. She always sounded as if she was ready to engage in a fight or had just finished one. But this was just her. She didn't mean anything by it. And most times she was right.

There had always been this strong sexual tension between them. The relationship never went there, though. They made out a few times in the dirty bathroom and danced a few times more on the sweaty dance floor, but Suraya was raw and probably too raw for DJ. Between them, Suraya said, there was only love for the music, love for DJ's music. She couldn't take love from someone who'd already given her so much. Her love, she'd said mysteriously one day, was waiting to be found. A man who'd melt with her. Inside of her.

"That was a long time ago." DJ laughed.

"But you did!"

"Yes, I kicked them out, but we can't be like that. Not forever. People are going to keep coming."

"Coming for what? They don't need you to tell them that this started in the basement of the house you rented in college. That you couldn't pay the rent and you put together a mix that you thought would just get people in the neighborhood to come over and pay three dollars to dance for a bit. And then they came. And then they wouldn't leave. And then Melt was born." Suraya was rolling her eyes and listing these things on her fingers as she went.

"So what do you propose we do?"

"We close it off. We cut them out."

"Cut them out?" DJ laughed at this idea, but really he'd thought of it before. "What, you want this to be a compound?"

"I want this to be our house. Where we love. Where we love one another and make love to one another," Suraya said dramatically, holding her hands out over the crowd in front of the club. "And no one can try and take it away. Can try and copy it. Make it what they want it to be."

"We can't stop it, Ray," DJ said. "It's already gone. Maybe we need them to tell others our message."

"Has that ever worked with them before?"

"DJ?" An anxious voice called from behind. Suraya and then DJ turned sharply to see Elliot walking toward them.

"Speak of the devil," Suraya mumbled.

"Hey, man," DJ said, getting up and wiping tiny pieces of concrete from his hands.

Suraya remained seated. She looked out over the front of the club with purpose.

"Look, I don't know if you still want to do the interview, but—" Elliot started.

"It's no problem. I wanted to come here, have a good time and experience it, see it all and help tell your story the way you want people to hear it."

"Humpf," Suraya complained before clearing her throat.

DJ looked from Elliot to Suraya and then back again.

"Hey, Ray," he started, "I have someone I want you to meet."

Again, Suraya's lack of concern was both visible and audible, yet she turned a bit to see Elliot and pass a fake smile.

"Elliot, this is Suraya. She's one of our loyal family members. Been here really since we started the club," he said. "She's the flavor of this place. The queen."

Suraya's frown slid into a grin. She got up from the ground slowly and shook Elliot's hand.

"Of course," Elliot said. "I see the crown. I saw you on the dance floor, too. You're something."

"What newspaper are you from? And what are you writing about?" Suraya pushed.

"I'm with the *L.A. Times* and I'm—"

"Look, tell the people to get into their own thing. To stop trying to duplicate our Melt and make their own. Follow their own rhythm and see what it says. That's the freedom. The tick inside of them. They can't take what he made and make it their own. They need their own." Suraya's face was full of passion now. She was so close to Elliot that DJ saw that they were the perfect melt pairing. His shoulders were three inches above hers. And her waist bent right between his legs.

"It's a great message," Elliot said uneasily, "but I think there's more—"

"Suraya, take Elliot to the dance floor," DJ said quickly.

"What?" They both asked before putting their hands up in protest. Suraya stepped over and stood beside DJ.

"Really. I want you to take him to dance." He nudged her. "To show him what you're saying."

"But I can't dance," Elliot said.

"And I can't dance with him," Suraya jumped in. "Passing me off like I'm some kind of…"

As Suraya complained, DJ grabbed Elliot and pulled him to the side.

"Is that your girl? She's all upset and…," Elliot asked.

"She's not my girl."

"But she at least likes you. I saw how she was looking at you in there. Hey, I don't want to get involved in this. I came here to write my story and—"

"You're here, Elliot," DJ said, sobering while grabbing Elliot by the shoulders the way a father would his son. "In that e-mail you sent, you wrote about wanting to be here. About loving the music and listening and wanting to share that with the world. Well, this is it. You're here. And no amount of listening and watching is going to get you the story you want. You have to feel this shit, man. You have to get out there and let it rattle you. Then maybe it can…" He saw Suraya standing behind Elliot, her arms crossed, her eyes threatening departure.

"Maybe what?"

"Maybe it can free you."

DJ was back in his booth.

The crowd exploded into a frenzy. DJ almost never closed the party and they knew this must have been some kind of special treat. Men pulled off their shirts and women hiked up their skirts. They bounced and waved with the first roll of drums and then, through the crowd came Suraya, strutting and pulling Elliot by his shirt to the middle of the dance floor.

Elliot's face was so red the people standing around stopped to gawk at him. He waved at them nervously, pretending to be following the music.

Suraya gazed up at DJ in his perch. Her eyes were red and her thick black mascara was running down her cheeks.

"I love the music," she mouthed to him, knowing he'd never understand. "And I love you."

It was gospel with funk. DJ was invoking the spirit. Something from beneath the floorboards. Something that rattled the room and forced folks to back away from Elliot and Suraya in the center of the stage. Elliot was shaking his head. Suraya grabbed him by the throat and pulled him into her breasts where her heart was ticking with the bass of the funk.

"You feel that?" She spat and pounded herself into him. "That's it. That's fucking it." She pounded and nearly pushed him off his feet.

Elliot turned to walk away, off the dance floor, but Suraya caught him by his belt and pulled his backside to her crotch. She shimmied as the gospel faded into salsa.

The crowd hollered and laughed.

"Feel it," she whispered into Elliot's ear from behind. "Feel it and let go."

Elliot, not knowing what else to do and sure he'd lost his backpack holding his digital recorder somewhere on the dance floor, closed his eyes like he sometimes did when he was alone in his baby blue room in Nebraska and dreaming of being here. He followed the waves of the Melt as they crashed inside him.

DJ pulled off his headset and looked down at Elliot. He saw his hips thrusting to the floor and Suraya on his back, pushing him and edging him on. Fists were pumping in the air.

The man was coming up then. His red dreadlocks flicked and pointed up toward the ceiling like arrows as he turned in just a second and twisted to face the woman.

He grabbed Suraya's arms and turned them so her back would come into him. The headdress fell to the floor and she bent to pick up it. He kicked it away and snatched her hands into his.

"You don't need that," he said, spreading his legs out to the drums and crossing his arms over her back.

He was grinding now. And Suraya was pushing back up at him, ticking and feeling his pulse. She'd forgotten about her headdress.

The salsa moved to something slower. An African song with a thin guitar being plucked in the background.

Elliot melted into the chords and didn't care to remember one bit of it.

"I guess we'll do the interview in the morning," DJ said, yawning in Elliot's face as they walked out of the emptying club.

"I'm done," Elliot answered.

"What?"

"I have what I need."

"But what about your questions?" DJ noticed that Elliot wasn't carrying his backpack.

"There's nothing you can tell me that hasn't already been said. The problem is you can't record this. The people will have to come here for themselves. They'll have to feel this."

"That's righteous, man," DJ said, gripping Elliot's hand. "Hey, do you need a ride to the airport in the morning?"

Elliot grinned and looked up toward the roof.

"I'm probably not going anywhere for a while now," he said. "I have a date with a queen."

KNOCK

New York night bodies. Sweating and glowing in a musk created by the most human of activities. Two or three, sometimes four. In a bed engaged in ceremony. Filled with red passion. Digging and opening. Seeking only to be remembered in the mind.

But, the secret is, there are nights when there is nothing. Nothing but empty space in the big bed. A human mind. Trying to forget red passion. Trying to move on.

I close my eyes. I see a mix of dark shadows of black and blue and grey. Sleep would be easier than this isolation. But I chose it. I chose it. Too many bodies in the bed are heavy on the mind. Sleep is nowhere near.

Still, maybe all red hearts aren't aware of the blackout.

A loud pound rattles the door.

My eyes open to light in the night of my domicile. There is an intruder.

Who could it be? A body wrapped in lace or fishnet? Better yet two bodies: one in lace and one in fishnet? Wet in the middle? Seeking only to be remembered in the mind? Doormen. Security. Pass codes and keypad entry. Red passion knows its way around all of this protection of the home and mind. It's sneaky. It's desirable in its sneakiness.

In the past, I never cared. Now, I want to know why. Now, I want to know more, to experience more.

But the questions only bring action. Action allows for open doors. And then open legs. And then sweat in rivers until sunrise. And wasn't that sneaky, too? Action isn't love. And that's what I want to know.

I cannot. I turn over and try to sleep again.

The door rattles again. No more sweat. I won't answer. I see legs over my head. Saliva on breasts. There's purring in my ear as I push until it reaches a sigh and then a stiff body beneath me. It is done. But I am back where I began. Empty. No more. I won't answer. I roll over again for sleep. This is the commitment. I am desperate. No man can be poised when he seeks solitude from the red passion. Just committed. To change. For more.

The emptiness spreads over. Maybe the potential intruder waits in lace or fishnet or maybe she has retreated while wearing both.

Sometimes a public life is a curse. It affords no time for real growth. Still, we chase it like it's a ruler to measure the maturity of a fine wine. And I have chased it. I have been to Vegas and seen fights and great fighters—royal from the first seat in the front. Mike Tyson and Lennox Lewis. Roberto Durán and Sugar Ray Leonard. I've seen faces shattered by punches. Witnessed the obliteration of men and cheered as blood came so close to my skin. Taken pictures for magazine spreads in the rows set up like church pews around a ring where men are battered and red passion flies from the nostrils after devastating punches. Their measure in the ropes. My measure outside. A knockout by way of flashing bulbs.

When the rapping at the door begins again, I am dreaming that I am fighting. I am in the ring with Muhammad Ali. It is the "Thrilla in Manila." Only the thrill is gone. Ali is punch drunk on his feet. We are both old men doing something that looks like bobbing and weaving, but really we're trying to remain erect. We know we should've quit this a long time ago.

Half awake, I don't know not to answer the door. Instinct pulls me from my bed.

The knocking must stop. Across the cold living room floor, I shuffle step, pattern my feet before one another like I am shadowing Ali in the ring. Tired but curious. This knocking isn't familiar. There is no memory of it. It's new.

I blink sleep from my mind and stand at the door.

Two more knocks.

The source is beautiful through the peephole.

But it's so late. Or is it early?

The beautiful knocker is smiling. I didn't recognize the knock, and the smile is from a face I'd only seen on the elevator. In the lobby. In the garage. A neighbor. But there was no cup for sugar in her hand. No invitation to knock after midnight. Just a smile that crept up my back and whispered, "Let me in."

I open the door.

I am about to say something friendly while making an inquiry, but the body pushes past me bouncing, hips swaying like women do.

Inside, she turns and smiles again. She's tricked me.

She laughs like there's music in her voice and says, "Have any wine? A little cheese?"

"No."

"No to what?"

"The cheese, I had a party last night. I do have some fruit, crackers," I say, interested, but also wondering how I became involved in such an exchange. I am in my cream linen night pants. No shirt. No shoes.

She bounces and glides to the couch. Her ass is tight. Sitting at the very top of blue jean shorts with red rhinestones over the pockets, the kind smart women can only wear at home or to take out the trash seemingly innocently to seduce an ignorant man. I know the trick, but the exposed chocolate back at the top of the shorts and the long leans legs at the bottom that lead down into red leather stilettos has my heart pumping thick blood quickly into my pants.

She sits on the couch, kicks off her shoes and crosses her legs.

"Bet you have wine, though." She cuts me off and laughs again to let me know that she knows who I am. That I am on the list.

"Who are you?" I ask, standing before her on the couch. "I've seen you around here before but—who are you?"

"I'm Ericka. Yes, I live in this building. I walk an invisible dog on a leash. The girls are so cute with their dogs and their pretty purses and, given that all of them think that I am a model who should carry a miniature dog, I went to the store and got the next best thing. It's a great conversation piece. I stand with the other ladies wearing our dark sunglasses and our fur coats with short skirts, our Prada purses and Louis Vuitton bags, our Coach shoes and even the Hermès purses. And we sit in the park. I pet my dog." She looks at me. "What? Why are you looking at me like that?"

"That was a lot of information."

"You asked who I am. You didn't give me a word limit."

Even with the extended answer, the knowledge of who she is and what has brought her to my door, I am still conjuring up questions. Who is she to demand wine from me in the middle of the night? How does she know that I didn't already have someone there, lying in my bed limp? Someone who's already had the wine and is emerging from my shower, calling my name and wrapped in my robe? Maybe she doesn't care. Maybe she hasn't noticed. I have two rules: One. I don't escort a woman to my door. Two. She must be gone by sunrise.

I look into Ericka's face to discover why she is so beautiful. Is it in parts or the entire construction? Her chin is balancing a dimple and her cheekbones are high and made for pictures. I almost lose my breath.

"Look, I'm going to put a shirt on and then get the wine."

"No, Maxwell. No shirt." Her eyes scan like a laser over my chest. I have to grin. "And choice on the wine?"

"You have them all. You're on the list. Right?"

"Right."

Living in a building with affluent residents leaves no secrets. Notices on mailboxes, parties, guests, entries and exits were all invitations for information to be collected. The women knew who'd gotten what shoe on what day in the mail. The men know whom the new business titans are, who to invite to lunch, and who to fuck. It was prep school with mortgages and access to the elite.

The recent chatter in the hallway is about me making The Reserve wine list again. The winery has an exclusive list of tasters selected to serve their wines in private residences. There are presidents and heads of state. The prime minister of the United Arab Emirates is

THE LOVE I KNOW

on the list for The Popular Reserve. There are also directors from Hollywood and a myriad of interesting characters. F. Gary Gray is on the list. Halle Berry. Kara Walker. And then there are the A-list New Yorkers. MacArthur Fellows scholars, authors and music types in Alphabet City. Designers in SoHo. And me.

Every month a new box arrives in the lobby. The doorman buzzes me and asks if he should bring it upstairs.

"I think you should pick the wine," I say to Ericka. "I don't have a taste for anything right now. I had a party last night."

"I know." She stands and follows me into the kitchen.

"You heard the noise? I apologize. My friend Oscar plays the djembé drum and often, when Melloui begins his painting, which he does at each of my parties, Oscar has to start with his playing." I point to the dying seahorses drying on a canvas tacked to one of the walls in my living room. Melloui is one of the artists in my gallery. Oscar is an old friend who carries a djembé drum wherever he goes.

"No. You told me earlier. Remember?"

The conversation turns to the seahorse and why Melloui has been painting so many the entire year.

In the kitchen, Ericka stands over my shoulder as I read labels on the wine case.

I don't know if I can smell her or if I just want to. If I am imagining the spring breeze blowing gently behind me with a promise of an indiscriminate mix of pollen from wherever. I am from Georgia and I miss the sweet pollen showers of spring that never seem to blow in New York City.

"I have the Reserve," I announce during a pause. "And the Popular."

"Which do you like best?" Ericka asks. Her voice is all West Coast. Maybe Oregon. She looks too delicate, too untouched to be from Los Angeles. She leans down and her Brown breasts sit over my shoulder looking like droplets of pudding still cooling. Not one mark or streak.

"The Popular is the obvious pick. But I prefer the Reserve."

"Guess we have a winner. The Reserve it is," Ericka says and stands. Suddenly I wish I'd taken longer to make a selection. If she was any other woman in fishnets or lace showing up at my door so late, I would've pulled her breast into my mouth and sucked her nipple until she begged me to fuck her right there in front of the rack. But I know somehow that she is not one of those women, and I am trying not to be that man.

"We need music now," Ericka says, walking barefoot back into the kitchen as I uncork the wine. She's plucked two red wine glasses from the counter. She seems at home, like she's navigated my space before. I wonder if she lives in the same unit. I imagine her living above or below, listening to women moan into the night. For the first time, I wonder who else has heard.

I pick up the remote and Miles Davis plays from every angle.

We find seats on the couch in the living room. I am on one side of a chestnut leather couch my decorator had shipped from Italy and I hate.

Ericka is on the other side of the couch holding the glass of wine. Her feet are tucked into the back seams of the couch.

We listen to the music for a while.

"Every Black man should play Jazz. Right? Be a musician. Don't you think?" Ericka asks.

"I've never thought of it," I say. "I don't think we can all be musicians. It's a talent. A skill. Why do you say that?"

"My ex-boyfriend, Salah, wanted to be a lawyer. I supported him. Paid his tuition. I went to his graduation and everything. Two weeks later, he decides he wants to be a chef," she says. "Ridiculous. The thing is, I knew he wouldn't be a good lawyer. He could hardly win a debate with me about which movie to see. He lacked passion about anything. Even me. Musicians have passion. Jazz musicians have more heart than the rest of us. Miles. Listen to him. He pours all his heart into one thing. That's what we need. More brothers who aren't afraid to pour all their heart into one thing."

"Miles was also a woman beater," I point out right before being angry that I had. There was no purpose. I was just showing off, letting her know I knew something about him.

"Not that part. Surely, you know I don't mean that part." She said without punishing me for the dumb move.

"Okay, well, let's pretend that every Black man is a Jazz musician. What then?

"Can you imagine?" She laughs. "Harlem would be magical. All of Africa would be alive."

We sit and listen some more. "Doxy" fades away and "Tutu" begins to play.

I look at Ericka and wonder what she knows about Jazz. She's bopping her head to Miles's last great cut. Well, it could be argued, but does she know what this is? Or is she like many of the other women who can point out Miles and say they love Jazz but don't know the music.

"Like you," Ericka says, looking back at me. "You're like a Jazz musician. You play passionately."

"Excuse me?"

"I watch you walking into the building. How you walk. Talk on your phone. Wave. It's all music. Like a rhythm to it. You're in your own world. You don't notice anything around you. Not even me." She repositions one of her legs from the seams and stretches it down toward me on my end of the couch.

"Is that why you're here?"

"I'm here for the wine and music," she pauses. "Yeah. The company, too."

"I'm glad, I guess," I say with no control.

She looks closer at me and in her eyes I see that she knows that I know that she knows that she's got me somehow. She kicks out her other leg and her foot is on my thigh.

"How'd you get on the list?" she asks.

"I know the owner."

She laughs. Tips her head backward into the couch like it's the funniest joke she's ever heard. "Nonsense. If that was the case, everyone in Maxwell's first grade class would be on the list. His classmates from Morehouse College. Come on. That's not it. There's something special about you."

"It's not wise to talk about yourself. People know what they know. They believe what they want to believe."

"I know some things about you. There's this blog this girl keeps about art dealers in Manhattan. You have the largest collection of Basquiat in the city. You knew him."

"Maybe that's why I'm on the list. The blog," I say.

I notice that her glass is empty and lean over to pour more.

"You need more wine, too," she says.

"I'm fine."

"We can't toast if you don't have a full glass. It's bad luck."

"I've never heard that. And what are we toasting to?"

"Well, it's true. Have some more. Why not? You're at home. You're with a beautiful woman. It's early. We'll toast to the night."

We finish one bottle and I don't remember how we get to the third. Talking probably. Laughing.

Through the dance we do, exploring and withholding, I learn Ericka is a stockbroker. A beautiful stockbroker who I keep thinking could've been a model. Listening to her talk and admiring her beauty: I wonder how I could've missed her. I can only think that I've probably categorized her. This talk. Laughing at 2 a.m. and not knowing where anything is going, but cool about it. A toast to the night. We should've crossed paths before. I'm mad that we haven't. I've missed it.

She's on the floor, sitting between my legs now, drawing circles on my inner thigh. I don't know if it's an invitation for something more or maybe to tease and I don't care. I don't want to ask or push and give her an inclination to leave.

"Women talk about you," she says. "They want to know things."

"What do you want to know?" Without thinking, I begin to stroke her hair. The music has changed to John Coltrane. It feels right.

She leans into my stroke.

"What every woman wants to know. If you're ready.

"Ready for what?" I reply.

"Life. Commitment to a woman. Marriage. Ready to be a child's father." She looks right into my eyes. "Are you?"

"Are you their detective? Their representative?" I ask.

"No. I'm the one who dares to ask. I figure it's better to get the messages from the writer. Not the readers."

Coltrane is furious in the speakers. I finish my wine. Remember the fishnets over my couch. No one had ever asked me such a thing so directly. It's all illusion and suspicion. Games. Careful games that repeat and recycle. No one wanting a broken heart.

"Are you ready? Really ready?"

"I'm tired of where I am," I say, turning the wine glass in my hand. "Are you asking because you'd like to be a candidate?"

Ericka laughs and I feel like I can listen to her laughter forever. So full. So unapologetic in a quiet space on a quiet night. I wonder where her fake dog is.

"I don't even know you," she says. "I just wanted to know the answer. I'll tell you what I really want. I want to be on that list. The wine list."

"Oh, I see. And I'm the hookup?" I play with the chubby part of her ear that carries the weight of her silver earring.

"Yes." She laughs.

"Too bad, sugar. I can't help. You know as well as I that this year's listing is final."

"Really?" She nearly hums this to show that I've led myself to the correct conclusion.

"So, if it's not the grapes, then what is it?"

She dips her finger into her red wine and puts it into her mouth. "So sweet," she says. "Have you ever tasted the wine like this?"

"No."

She dips her finger again while trapping my eyes on hers, slides the wet finger into my mouth. She tickles my tongue gently but then thrusts back farther.

"Too sweet for one to enjoy all alone," she says and tries to remove her finger, but I won't let her.

If this is a game, I'm playing. I want her to stay in my mouth. I want to taste her. I clamp down playfully on her index finger.

"You keep my finger in your mouth and you won't ever be able to ask me to leave," she says.

I clamp down a little harder and she squirms. She climbs up on me with the wine glass in one hand and straddles me.

"You won't let go?" Ericka smiles.

I shake my head in objection.

She holds the wine glass over my head and threatens to pour.

I look up and clamp down again.

She lowers the glass right over my mouth and lets a little wine trickle into my mouth around her finger.

"Taste it," she nearly whispers.

I let go of her finger and she continues to pour the wine until drops are rolling down my chest.

She begins to lick and lick with her shorts hiked up in her ass.

I sit there watching and not moving, letting her control it all. She's masterful in her play. Deliberate but not promising the next lick will continue. I want to beg.

She drops the glass on the couch and watches me as she lowers her body to the floor between my legs again, moving slowly backwards like a cat. She unties my pants and pulls my penis out with both hands tight around the base.

"No, you don't—" I start, but she's faster.

She's in control. And somehow there's wine in her mouth and I feel it all over me. Cool. The feeling, sweet.

Don't want to but I beg. I beg. I beg.

My head falls back on the chestnut couch I don't like. My eyes close and roll back. I feel her nails clawing into my chest. Her tongue lapping up against my rigid skin. I see lace and fishnet. Women laughing and smiling. Then crying. Reaching out to me. So many. A clock. Ericka at the door. The rhinestones on her ass. I wonder how long I've been awake. Or am I sleeping? Something rattles in me. Clangs from my knees to my throat. The nails on my chest tear my skin and I explode. I am dreaming.

All around us Pharoah Sanders and Coltrane are playing the live recording of "Introduction to My Favorite Things."

We're in the shower. The steam rises all around us.

Ericka's ear is pressed into my chest. I hope she can hear my heart beating.

"It'll be morning soon," she says. "And we'll be clean."

"Where will we go?" I ask.

"Anywhere."

THE BOWL OF ICING

Light knows no humble way and has no respect for dreamers or men who wish to lie in state when night has gone away.

Humphries knew this, but still he tried with loud sighs and a pillow pulled right over his head to stop the inevitable shine clawing its way into his bedroom at sunrise.

He'd been having that dream again. That dream about her. And he wanted to remain there—or to go back. He wasn't really sure yet if he was all the way awake or half asleep but he had the sense that the gold glowing at his eyelids was a sign of a new day penetrating his old dream. He wanted more time with her. He wanted to feel that thing, that tickling in his gut when she laughed at him jumping through the sprinklers in the backyard. But she was gone now. Her laugh. Her kiss. Her smile in his eyes. Gone. She could only live in his dreams. So on some mornings, mornings like these, after that dream, so nice and cruel at the same time, left him wanting more. Humphries wished that somehow he could pull her through into his world with the light, find an opening somehow, and let her live again.

But there could be none of that. The wet green grass and her laugh almost seemed like another life now. Another world. He was a boy then. Now he's a man. And Humphries was learning fast that such splendor could only be truly enjoyed in memory. A new day meant new time that took him further from this memory. Further from her and the time they'd shared. Time used. Time spent. Time relentless in placing more distance between them every day that the light tiptoed through the spaces in the blinds, streaked along the bedroom walls, seeped up under his pillow and threatened to pull back his eyelids with invisible fingers that went everywhere.

"Made a cake last night. Five-flavored in a bundt pan. Figured you'd want some. It's Friday."

Sundae Brown hardly turned her back when Humphries walked into her shop at 7 a.m. She started speaking as she faced the cappuccino machine where she was blending a small cup for the woman with wet blond hair standing ahead of Humphries in line. Everyone inside knew who she was talking to.

"Don't know if I want any cake today, Sundae. I'll have my regular." Humphries was six-foot-three and his chin seemed to sit right over the woman's head in front of him, so his voice tunneled toward the front of the shop and bounced out all around maybe a little louder than he'd meant for it to be. He was used to always being the tallest kid in school. He was always at the back of the line as the class trailed down the hallway to the bathroom. He'd gotten his height from his grandfather, a man so dark, and so tall, and with a voice so deep, most people called him mean without ever having spoken to him.

Sundae was short and curvy. Brown like the skin of a sweet potato. She laughed a lot and made fast friends with anyone who walked into her coffee shop. While Humphries was sure they were around the same age—he'd never asked, but a few strands of grey hair at her temples and a healthy pucker in her cleavage relegated her to the thirty and up set in his head—Sundae seemed more mature, and wiser than any of the other women he knew. His mother might say that Sundae had "an old soul." She was always ready to take care of someone or give a smile from those shapely lips painted with a red that never seemed to fade.

She wasn't smiling at Humphries, though. She was frowning. She wiped her hand on her apron and said, "You saw my name up over the door outside?" Sundae pointed to the door behind Humphries when the woman ahead of him took her coffee and dropped her change into the tip jar before walking out.

Humphries stepped forward and hung his head low dramatically, prepared for a scolding. "Yes, I saw your name on the sign."

"So, you saw what it says underneath it?"

"Sundae Morning Coffee Shop—come get blessed," Humphries announced dryly as people setting up their laptops at tables near the bar tuned in and giggled at the show. It was a part of their morning routine. Sundae Morning Coffee Shop was the only business to survive the 2008 recession that smashed the merchants in the lobby of Humphries' modish condo development that had promised D.C.'s budding Black professional business elite a "Live-Work-Play" experience in the dramatically gentrified downtown urban corridor. As the retro boutique owner, high-end jewelry dealer, hair dresser and band fitness trainer closed their doors, residents flocked downstairs to save Sundae by getting a morning cup of coffee or tasting one of her cakes that some of the formerly single female residents claimed had aphrodisiac qualities. During a time of such uncertainty, when the new MBAs and old top floor titans knew not one promise that could be kept in a career that they'd made their life, Sundae was a familiar and friendly smile they wouldn't let go of.

"Exactly, I'll bless you," Sundae repeated, pointing first at herself and then at Humphries with the respective pronouns. "So, why won't you let me do my job?"

"I'm sorry, Sundae. I just don't feel like having cake. Bad morning. Gonna be a bad day." Humphries exhaled deeply, struggling to release the last memory of his dream. "Wish I didn't have to get out of bed this morning."

"Oh, you have to get some of this cake now. All this sad talk? Perfect time for some cake. Make you smile. Can't be sad when you're eating cake." Sundae walked to the little case where she displayed the cakes she'd made with her mother's recipes each week. Shortcake, Pineapple Upside Down, Lemon, German Chocolate, 7UP. There was every color, shape and taste.

Ending his morning run down Georgia Avenue a little later than usual, Humphries eagerly headed toward Sundae's shop. It was a cold Sunday morning and he needed a cup of her signature spicy hot chocolate, but remembered that she didn't open on Sundays. He went to the shop anyway, hoping peeking inside would warm him. To his surprise, the lights were on and Sundae was inside smiling with her red lips and Brown skin. Along with a small group of women Humphries recognized from the building, she was sitting at a table mapped with slices of cakes. Humphries figured it was one of the cake parties he'd seen on fliers in the elevator. He pressed his ear against the cold glass window. The women were laughing.

"This cake, the Red Velvet," Sundae said, holding up the crimson slice with cream cheese icing. Humphries thought he could taste by looking at it. "It's the lover's cake. No couple can argue after eating it. No man can turn you away." She handed the slice over to the women and they passed it around, digging into it with their forks as they moaned and sighed in agreement. "The Tiramisu…" She held up another plate with a little brown square on it. "…is the cake of the morning after. After brunch, you feed this to your beloved and let him lick the crumbs from your fingertips." She passed the plate around to the same effect as the last.

"Now, this one is the Sock-it-to-Me. It's the way you let him know you like him. It's solid. It's traditional. Sweet. He'll call his mother and tell her you made it for him. She'll tell him he's found a wife."

One of the women whose wedding Humphries would be invited to a few months later squealed when the slice of Sock-it-to-Me met her tastebuds. "Lord Jesus, Sundae! You need to make a cake like this for my man," she said.

Sundae stopped her just as all the other women were about to agree. "No, it's important that he taste the cake made by your hands. Most women have forgotten this art form. The cake has everything you need—sugar, flour, eggs—hell, some have vegetables."

The women laughed and Sundae looked up at the window to see Humphries. She jumped up and waved for him not to walk away.

"You want to come inside?" She asked, poking her head out the door.

The women turned and looked at him interested and nudging one another.

"No. I thought you were open," Humphries said. "I'll come back tomorrow morning." Sundae smiled. "I can make you something," she said. "Get you some cake. What do you need?" Humphries backed up. "I'll come back in the morning,"

"Sundae, I don't want any cake—"Humphries tried to stop Sundae again, "I come back on Monday morning when the shop was actually open," but she waved him off the way a mother does to her son clawing at her apron for cherry pie before it's cooled. "Nonsense. Look, it's on the house." She cut a healthy piece from the freshly made Bundt and slid it onto a saucer that had a little boy in red trousers playing with a kite painted in its center.

"No icing?" Humphries pointed out when she set the cake on the counter beside his black coffee.

"It's a Pound Cake!"

"But I like icing. You know that. Can't have cake without icing."

"How you go from not wanting any cake to wanting icing?" Sundae laughed and leaned into the counter in a way that made her breasts dangle over the cake. "Fine!" She popped back up just as Humphries was feeling his imagination wander down the split of her cleavage. He'd always thought she was a beautiful woman. Maybe not his type. But definitely beautiful. "You're actually in luck!"

Sundae walked back to the display case and scooped something onto the saucer beside the cake.

"It's my cream cheese frosting," she said to Humphries when she returned to the register. "I know you like icing, so I made a little special for you. Just promise you won't eat them together—the cake and the icing. The icing will make the cake too sweet. You gotta really taste it on its own."

"But I love icing. It makes things easier to eat."

"Hum…" Sundae nodded. "You know my grandmother had one rule about icing—you can have as much of it as you like, but only on special occasions."

Humphries handed Sundae a bill that required change she knew he wouldn't take. As their hands met, Sundae tickled the center of

Humphries' palm with her middle finger. He grinned but quickly moved his hand away rather boyishly for a man of his size and stature. She inquired a few times about who Humphries was dating, asked why in the three years he'd been coming to her shop she hadn't seen him with one woman. The answer was so simple it seemed like a lie: there hadn't been any.

"You have a good day," Sundae said slowly and softly, looking into his eyes in a way that was so friendly it was seductive. "Remember, I'm here to bless you."

"Thank you."

Like Sundae, when Humphries smiled, people responded. Even when he was down. Even when he wasn't sure. Even when he was confident that failure was imminent, he knew that a smile, simply curling up the sides of his mouth would yield the best results. It was how he made his way in the world. A full scholarship to North Carolina A&T for undergrad. He'd pledged the best fraternity, was at the top of his business class, and got internships every summer that took him all over Asia. He went on to Howard University for a free MBA and got the best job right out of grad school. A dream salary at the largest merchandiser in the Nation's Capital. He'd smiled so much the whole time that no one could ever have imagined that he was the first in his family to even think of finishing high school and going to college. His father had been killed in a bar fight three months before he was born. His mother had been addicted to crack for most of his life, but gave it up only to die with a needle in her arm when Humphries was seventeen. He was still smiling, though.

This made Humphries the best salesman at Pitch Company. The top in his region almost every quarter. Old guys, young guys, White guys, they all asked what his secret was. Humphries would smile and nod like he was accepting a compliment. Maybe he'd say something in Mandarin and bow his head graciously.

Standing at the floor-to-ceiling window in his corner office, Humphries looked out into the start of day. People marching to somewhere. Smiling and talking on cellphones. He fingered his suspenders and wondered what she might look like walking around with these people in the crowd. Would she look up at the window and see him? Wave? Call him and say she was coming up to his office? What would she think of his red suspenders? Did they make him look old? He was going for respectable. His mentor had sent them in the mail for Christmas. It was the only gift he'd gotten each year.

"Yo, Nupe!"

Humphries turned to find Jared walking into his office. Jared was his fraternity brother and the director of marketing. Their friendship was easy and smart. Humphries told Jared the image the brand needed so he could get a leg in with suppliers and distributors. Jared listened and turned that into success for both of them.

"Yo, Nupe!" Humphries responded, hugging Jared quickly as they shook hands in the way they had been taught by their big brothers.

Jared sat in the brown leather chair beside Humphries' desk and leaned back confidently, crossing his legs the way a successful man could.

"So, what's the plan, man?"

"Plan?"

"Tonight? Your birthday? Don't play with me. I already got the night off with Karen. She ain't gonna be tripping. I told her it's Friday and a nigga ain't coming home!"

"Birthday?" Humphries looked at his computer screen at the date. How could he have missed it? Well, he never cared about it. But he never missed it either. Suddenly, he heard her voice as clear as if she was standing behind him: "I am far away, but there is nothing that can keep me from you—not if you try. Not if you really try not to forget me. I'll remember you always." He felt a kiss on his cheek and turned to see her. Maybe she'd come in with the light. But there was just the window. The people walking in the street.

"Nupe, you all right?" Jared looked at Humphries concerned. "You look like you've seen a ghost." He laughed a little.

"I'm fine. I just… I guess I kind of forgot that it was my birthday."

"Getting old, huh? Don't trip, bruh. At least you don't have a wife and two badass kids. The way I see it, if you made it to thirty-seven and you're alone, that's a reason to celebrate!" Jared raised a pretend glass in a pretend toast.

Humphries frowned at Jared. "You love Karen. Why do you always trip out on her?"

"Yeah, I do. And I ain't shit without her, but tonight! Tonight! It's all about us!—no homo!" Jared said, laughing. "So, what's the plan?"

"Plan?"

"Have you been listening? Tonight? The plan for us. Going out. Partying! I don't have a curfew." he reminded.

Humphries remembered the kiss on his cheek. "Nah, man. I can't. I just need to relax. Go home and sit for a while. I've been stressed," he said.

"Stressed? You're in the lead. Your clients call you. There are rumors of them making you VP next month. What's the stress?"

"You wouldn't understand."

"No, I understand," Jared said. "You need some pussy."

"Oh, Jesus," Humphries murmured.

"Now, I done set you up with Melissa—from Georgia—booty like an onion," Jared started counting off on his fingers. "Then I set your Black ass up with White Jenny from South Carolina—booty like an onion. It may be fake; but it's shaped like a nice round onion. Both of them went back to Karen and told her how you never even called them back after the first date."

"So?"

"So, what's up with that? You're gonna have to do something soon or people are going to start saying—well, you know what they'll start saying. I mean, what's the deal?"

Humphries looked at his friend. "This has nothing to do with needing pussy or being gay. I'm good. Just not in the mood right now."

"What about that thick chick at the coffee shop in your building?"

"Sundae?"

"Yeah! You're always talking about her. Why don't you holler? See what the deal is?"

"Holler? I don't think so. We're not the same. She's not exactly my type."

"Your type is alive, brother. Breathing!"

"I like our relationship the way it is. Plus, she has the shop. She's doing her thing. She's busy. I don't want to interfere with that. Not with my stuff."

"The hell you don't. The way you be talking about those juicy titties. Shit, you need to hit that. She don't need to be your type for that."

"I wouldn't do that to her. And it's not really about her not being my type. It's more like she's a real woman. She has her thing going on. You know? I don't want to distract her from her dream."

"I don't even know what you just said," Jared said dismissively, getting up from his seat to leave. "All I know is that you'd better get it together. Like before eight o'clock tonight when I get to your place. The freak train waits for no one. And I'm catching the train."

They hugged and shook hands again before Humphries was alone in the office with his thoughts.

He'd met Jared his freshman year at A&T. Just a year after his mother died. Jared was cool, didn't ask Humphries anything about his past, and seemed to know not to. He kept talking about pledging his grandfather's fraternity. How it had always been his dream to do it freshman year—just like his grandfather and father had. At some point, he started talking about Humphries pledging with him. Humphries smiled and Jared offered to pay for it. Insisted. Humphries said he'd pay him back one day and he did. A year after being at Pitch, he told the president of the company about his old friend who knew a lot about new trends in marketing.

Jared was always on Humphries about having a good time. He was the one who talked Humphries into moving downtown. He'd picked out the red Maserati and found him every date he'd ever had. He said Humphries needed to loosen up. "Bust some skins." Humphries was no virgin, though. There'd been that summer in Thailand. Those girls in the freshman dorm after he pledged. The White girl with the red hair in grad school. He kept thinking that Jared was wrong, but knew a part of his message, though roughly shared, was right. But how could he? How could he move on from her? Leave her there? In his memory? He'd been in love and lost her in a few hours when he wasn't paying attention. When he was dreaming that a future without her might be brighter than their dark past. But he learned that light is a force that destructs. That ruins. That takes away chances. He wanted to be all she ever needed. To save her. But how quickly had she withered away when he wasn't looking?

He remembered her smile. A smile just like his own. And that reminded him of Sundae and her cake. First thing in the morning and she had already been smiling and holding his birthday cake. She was always so nice to him. He wanted to be nicer to her. Maybe invite her up to his place for a drink after she closed the shop. Maybe they'd kiss. They'd bake a cake together. She'd show him how to make icing and warn him not to eat the entire bowl. He'd sit on the floor and cry with the bowl between his legs. She'd ask him what was wrong and he'd finally say it. Finally to someone. He missed his mother. Maybe Sundae would come pick him up off the floor, hold all of him in her arms, and say she could take care of him. She'd listen to the story about the day he was going to take the college entrance exam and how his mother begged him to stay at home and said she needed him. She said she couldn't make it that day without him. She was sick. Humphries smiled and said she'd be fine. She was doing better. Right? He was going to take that test so he could make things better forever. Make each day like sunshine. He left her in the living room. That's where he found her, too. With the needle in her arm. Sundae would smile and lull him to sleep. Sleep. Finally. Real rest with the truth free and in this life.

Right there in his office, Humphries thought for the first time that maybe it wasn't his mother he was trying to take from his dreams and into his life. Maybe it was the truth about how he'd lost her. Maybe if he told Sundae that night with icing she'd say it was okay. She'd forgive him. She'd watch him sleep. And when the sun came up, she'd feed him breakfast. She'd remind him to love again.

Humphries went home and rewarded his long day with a tall scotch. He sat on the couch and looked at a black television screen as he sipped. He'd been born on this day—thirty-seven years ago.

He'd spent a lot of time becoming who he was. He changed his name before he went to college. He learned perfect English and perfect Mandarin. He knew what scotch to buy. How to present and defend. He'd done everything he promised he would. There was no difference between him and men like Jared now. He could stand with them and feel like something. Really feel like a man. Not some worthless drug user who'd die all alone on a bar room floor before he ever met his only child. But there, right there was the thing that he didn't have. He was all alone in the world. He had everything, but no one to share it with.

He remembered the conversation he'd had with the grief counselor a few years after his mother died. He'd told her about the voices. The dreams. She advised him to limit and decrease his talks with the deceased, the one he'd lost. To remain healthy he had to leave that conversation and stop confusing himself about whether or not he deserved love again. He had to know that he didn't cause it. He didn't hurt anyone.

"You are mourning, Humphries," she said. "That's all. And you will be mourning for a long time. Until you let that go."

The doorman called to announce that Jared was waiting downstairs. In a lunchtime text conversation he agreed to go out for a few beers after Jared begged and complained that it would be his only night of freedom for the month.

Humphries downed the scotch without a frown and headed for the door in his black suit that looked more akin to something someone would wear to a funeral than out for a drink on his birthday.

When he got down to the lobby he saw Jared standing beside the valet.

"You parked?" Humphries asked. "I told you I would come down. You want me to drive? On my birthday?"

"Not necessary, Nupe," Jared said. "We ain't going far."

"Where to? Kazoo's? The Pullman?" Humphries named a few of the bars on the street that were within walking distance and had the right clientele for their outing. There was a strip club around the corner but Jared had promised Karen that he would never go back to another strip club after one of the dancers had stolen his wallet and used his credit card to finance a trip to Rio de Janiero.

"Nah, not that far," Jared said, walking outside the building beside Humphries.

"Well, there isn't too much else around here. Just a few restaurants. I stopped going to that Malaysian spot. You know they got a seventy-three on their health department inspection last month and…" Humphries looked down the street and though it was already dark, he could see a woman standing on the corner with two children —one in a stroller, another holding onto the stroller and pointing at them. "Is that?" he paused to look some more.

"Yes, it's Karen," Jared approved.

"She's coming with us?"

"No, I'm going with her."

"What?"

"We're going out to dinner," Jared said, turning to his friend and looking directly into his eyes.

"Oh, I didn't know you invited—"

"You're not coming with us."

Noticing the serious look in Jared's eyes, Humphries asked, "What's going on? Something wrong?"

"No. Everything is going just as planned." Jared took Humphries by the arm and turned him away as Karen and the kids started walking along the side of the building toward the coffee shop. "Look, man, I want you to have some fun tonight. And I've set up a way to make sure of it—"

"I don't need you to set me up," Humphries said, cutting Jared off. He seemed nervous and pulled away from Jared.

"Hear me out now. It's not like those other times. This is someone you like. Someone you need."

"How do you know who I like? What I need?"

"I listen to you, brother." Jared turned toward the building and nodded to get Humphries to look.

Humphries turned around to find that they were standing in front of the coffee shop. The lights were dim. Sundae closed up at seven o'clock each night.

There was one table. One far in the back with a single candle lit in the center. A woman was sitting in one of the chairs with her back to the door. All Humphries could see were Brown shoulders and red straps.

"Who's that?"

"It's her—Sundae."

"For what? Why is she here?"

The men watched as Sundae pulled a little compact from beneath the table and checked her makeup.

"I asked her to be," Jared said. "For you. Dinner."

"Ah, man. I can't. She's—"

"She likes you, Humphries. She really likes you. I hardly had to ask her about tonight. I mentioned that it was your birthday and she—"

"But I just want to be alone and she—"

"It's just dinner, man. Go in there and talk to her."

"But—"

"If you don't go in there, she'll always wonder why you didn't. Why you left her."

Sundae closed the compact and slid it back into the purse on her lap.

Jared opened the door and the chime got her attention. She turned around excitedly waved Humphries in.

Humphries took a deep breath to rid himself of his worries. Something that felt like an eagle kicking off of his shoulders or a thick lock of hair being cut from the nape of his neck left him.

He started to walk into the shop and gave Jared the hug and handshake their big brothers taught them.

"Hey, I'll pay you back," Humphries said, smiling.

"No need to."

Humphries walked into the shop alone to see that the red straps held a short dress in place.

Sundae held out her arms and sang "Happy Birthday" when she hugged Humphries. It was the first time their touch went beyond the passing of a bill and a tickle in the palm of Humphries' hand. He didn't want to let go. He drew in her perfume and didn't realize that he'd closed his eyes until all he heard was her voice: "I'm so happy you came back."

Humphries opened his eyes, but didn't let her go. "What do you mean?"

"I only get to see you once each day. Today, I get to see you twice."

He hugged her again and peeked over her shoulder at the table. There, centered next to the candle was a bowl filled with white icing.

"I figured we could go without the cake tonight," Sundae said, turning to the bowl. "Just icing. You know my grandmother's rule."

Humphries laughed and they sat down to eat the entire bowl of icing over a conversation that would unite them forever. Humphries didn't mention his mother and the needle that time. But he would. Soon. And Sundae would take care of him.

FASTEN YOUR SEAT BELTS

I know that you are there. I feel you everywhere. I am glad that you touched me. Now I feel that there is no despair.

I feel you everyday. I am glad you feel and make me feel that way. I hope and know that you are everywhere and I feel it everyday.

I see you everywhere. I see you when you are not there. I see your smile that you wear. I see the birds in the air. I sing the songs that you still care. I hear the song inside my head. I remember what it was when you and I were close. Instead, we chose to hold each other you see and I feel you still even though you are not touching me.

So when it comes again and when I hold you in I will not let you go, you will always know that you were in tow.

Don't ever doubt you see. Know that I see you invisibly. Know that when you are there each day and know that in the things that we can say and nothing can express how I feel. I want you to know that you are and I feel the love that I need to know. The love that I would hope to show. So please stay and don't go. Know that it is there, love in tow.

And now that love has really began, this is now when love has to stand in front of others and in front of time. In front of trouble and in front of the mind, in front of feelings. In front of the show. For love must forever be in tow.

So now that you have heard my voice, now that you know that you are my choice, now that we have decided too that it is up for us and what we choose to do so fasten on yourself for a life ride, fasten on and choose not to hide.

Don't let doubt be your friend. Look inside and love again, instead of looking back, hold on to it and create the fact that we can love each other each and every day and we can create love and ask it to stay and it will if we both keep the faith you'll see and know that love is both from you to me and from me to you.

LOVE SOMEONE

I know by the feeling and the relationship to my mind
I can feel the soul of love flowing deep within my spine.
And I know that the reason that the sun shines in the night
It's because you are in my life girl and our love has taken flight.

So, anybody, anybody, anybody (long)
Would want to love you
Anybody, anybody want to love you
I know (long) I know, I know
Anybody want to love you.

So the feeling that I had of love that wouldn't last
It seems that you have placed it in a permanent love glass
I know that the time of your smile in my mind
Feeds my spirit, I am full and you're loving me with the wonderful wine.

Anybody, anybody, anybody would want to love you
Anybody, anybody (long) would want to love you
But you chose me so I know, I know (long)
Anybody would want to love you.

Each day, I know, each day, we grow
Each day love's in tow
Each day you are going to sow a love flower
But in my mind a cloud or mountain, that we can climb

No valley too low to get down
And make our love turn around
So anybody, anybody, anybody (long)
Ooh! Would want to love you.

THINGS TO REMEMBER

_____

_____

_____

_____

_____

_____

_____

_____

_____

_____

_____

_____

_____

_____

_____

_____

_____

FAVORITES

_____

_____

_____

_____

_____

_____

_____

_____

_____

_____

_____

_____

_____

_____

_____

_____

_____

FINISH THE SENTENCE

I know you love me _____

_____

_____

When I am hurt I want to _____

_____

_____

_____

Let's keep our relationship aline by _____

_____

_____

_____

I am open to loving you _____

_____

_____

_____

I will not bring up the past if _____

_____

_____

I want to go _____

_____

_____

When you introduce me to others, please _____

_____

_____

Forgive _____

_____

_____

I will never _____

_____

_____

I will not bring up the past if _____

_____

_____

LOVE NOTES

_____

_____

_____

_____

_____

_____

_____

_____

_____

_____

_____

_____

_____

_____

_____

_____

_____

Net proceeds of the sale of this
book go to:

Advocates for Grandparent Grandchild
Connection
A Non-Profit 501 (c) (3) Organization

Advocating that all grandparents and
grandchildren have a life-long bond.